NATASHA

ΠΑΤΑSHA

KATHIRESAN RAMACHANDERAM

PARTRIDGE
A Penguin Random House Company

To order additional copies of this book, contact
Partridge India
000 800 10062 62
orders.india@partridgepublishing.com

www.partridgepublishing.com/india

Contents

This book is dedicated to Natasha

PROLOGUE

There are in total eight million four hundred thousand precincts of hell of which twenty one precincts are the most dreadful of the dreadful and for a hundred years I was confined to this ghastly place. In all that time, never for a minute did she leave my side. She was with me always in my heart, in my mind and in my soul. I was her and she was me and we were one in mind, body and spirit. I had a name but to the mortal world I was known only as Amesha Spenta or the bountiful immortal.

At the appointed hour I was clad not in my usual turmeric robes. Instead I wore placid blue garbs that resonated the peace, calmness and serenity that had thus far eluded me. My sword Chandi was faithfully strapped to my back. I remember the day well and despite the hundred years that had gone by since my death every moment of my final hour remained clearly etched in my mind. She was seated in front of me, the living goddess; the highest goddess in the echelon. A small teak table stood impassively between us, the veneer on it still intact and it gleamed like it had just been given a fresh coat of varnish. She looked as radiant as ever her face aglow with the brightness of a thousand suns.

I saw tears well up in her eyes and stream down her cheeks like tiny beads of pearls. "I will be with you always and not for a moment will you feel mortal pain" she said to me in a reassuring voice. I didn't fear pain nor was I distressed by the prospect of being relegated to the blazing inferno below.

They came at the appointed hour, the emissaries of the death god Yama, miniature silhouettes with wings the size of my palms, fluttering around my body like tiny insects. I was tempted to swat away at them like one does a fly but caution prevailed and I restrained myself.

I kissed the goddess on the cheek and repeated the repentance prayer in her presence. Upon completion my body fell to the ground and my spirit was ejected from my listless body, propelled by a tiny gust of wind. In the minutes that followed my whole life flashed before me. I saw countless corpses and the sky was darkened by the outstretched wings of flighted vultures that swooped down pecking away at carcasses filling their bellies with the remains of discarded mortal flesh. I could hear the sound of bones being crushed between their beaks. "Repent" said a voice in my head and I repented.

I saw the dark fertile soil turn a blood red as the spilt blood of men and horses permeated through to the surface to give the soil a red hue. "Repent" said a voice in my head and I repented.

I saw the flames of death with women and children gathered around the pyres clinging to each other, huddling together crying, bereaving for lost husbands and fathers. Widows were so overcome with grief that some of them threw themselves into the funeral pyre. "Repent" said a voice in my head and I repented.

I had some reprieve when a platter of my favorite food appeared unannounced in front of me. I saw a table laid out with an assortment of dishes cooked with herbs and spices. I smacked my lips in anticipation of a scrumptious meal. My next of kin were giving a feast to commemorate my passing.

This was not my first passing nor would it be my last and over time I had grown accustomed to it. Two parts of the meal went to building my new body while the third went to the messengers of the Death God, Yama. The fourth was what I consumed. I relished my meal for I had to admit I was famished. When I was done, I washed it all down with a tall glass of red wine.

Once they had ingested the offering the messengers of Yama placed a noose around my head and tugged at my neck with the other end of the rope like horses pulled on the reins of a chariot. Yet again I felt a strong compulsion to resist but the voice in my head urged me to do nothing.

They dragged me through a desert and I felt the blistering heat of twelve suns beat down on me. There was not a drop of water in sight. I felt thirst, an unquenchable craving for water and I realized that the human body desires water more than any other form of sustenance and the longing for it sapped and sagged my spirit. "This is what it feels like to be thirsty" said the voice in my head and I nodded.

As we moved hinterland, I felt a cold wind touch my skin and as we continued the wind grew stronger and soon I was in the middle of a gale so strong that it would have torn the body of a mortal man apart in a matter of seconds. "This is what it feels like to be caught in the middle of a hurricane" said the voice in my head and I nodded.

The wind got colder and it was filled with bits of ice and frost that bit into all parts of my body. I shook and I shivered and I trembled in the blizzard. I forgot all about my thirst and became absorbed with the cold. As we continued the sordid wind brought with it, in addition to ice, sharp thorns that repeatedly pierced the flesh that clung to my spirit.

The emissaries of Yama then tugged at the noose around my neck and forced me to walk on a ground crawling with venomous snakes and scorpions. The track eventually led to a jungle filled with leaves as sharp as a razor's edge and as I walked through the jungle the leaves cut away at the skin that clung to my spirit and my spirit body was covered with cuts and abrasions. The journey lasted for days and as soon as I walked out of the dense cluster of knife like leaves, eagles gathered above my head and swooped down to peck away at the remaining skin and sunk their claws into the lingering flesh.

Eight and a half days into the journey, we reached the shores of the River of Tears which inspired sorrow and fear in all men. The flighted emissaries of the Death God dragged me across the river that was filled with mortal tears, constantly pulling and tugging at the noose around my neck. I swam when I could but I sank most of the time and all through the ordeal my skin was gnawed at by small fish with razor sharp teeth that tore away at my remains gathering tiny morsels in their mouths.

The journey continued for seventeen days and on the eighteenth day we reached the City of Jewels. It was a beautiful city of untold splendor, rich and divine, decorated with gems of immeasurable value. The residents of this city lived in exquisite grandeur and the buildings that lined the bejeweled pavements of the city were built from pure gold which glittered in the light of a blazing sun, inlaid with precious stones that dazzled with the seven colors of the rainbow. The sides of the pavements were lined with sculptured trees that were ornamented with flowers of inspired gold.

Those who had lived their lives without a need for valuable possessions do not feel the loss and they breeze through the city without care, while corrupted spirits feel lost and destitute and lament the loss of their wealth and their possessions. I journeyed through the city with ease glad to have left my worldly possessions behind.

We then reached the City of Sand where I was exposed to an un-abating sand storm. Winds travelling at speeds a hundred times that of a hurricane lifted the coarse sand off the ground hurling it at me from all directions at a velocity so intense that the tiny pellets went right through my flesh. I felt a recurrent stinging pain. "Repent" said the voice in my head and I repented.

Actions were easy enough. It was facing the consequences of one's actions that was difficult. All actions as per the laws of karma have consequences and the transition between death and rebirth is also a state of awakening. Among other things, the spirit realizes its faults and faces the consequences of its misdeeds. Those who have fulfilled their duties and have acquitted themselves honorably need not suffer for they die in peace secure in the knowledge that the journey to the hereafter or the afterlife would be a breeze.

We then journeyed to the Kingdom of Pain and there I was brought before its King, Jangama, who wore the face of terror and his eyes spoke of infinite horrors. He glared at me with crimson eyes set alight with unrequited rage. I returned his unwholesome gaze with an equally steely glare tempted to dislocate the gruesome head from the contorted body that it sat on but once again prudence prevailed.

The next city that we travelled to was the City of Terror, a city of dark and unyielding forests. During the journey I fed on offerings placed before an altar erected in my honor by my next of kin who continued with the death rites as required by custom, religion and tradition. While I ate the emissaries of Yama scorned and mocked in contempt.

In the following months my spirit travelled to the City of Sin where I was exposed to the seven sins of mortality and from there I was led to the City of Misery. Towards the end of the fifth month, before the beginning of the sixth, there was a ceremony held to commemorate my death and once again I feasted on the offerings that were laid before my altar.

The City of Misery is ruled by Vichitra, the younger brother of Yama, who resembled in appearance, a demon of gigantic proportions. Most spirits are instantly intimidated at the sight of Vichitra and shriek and cower in fright. With feeble voices they begged for mercy and clemency.

Finding none the spirits run in terror until they reach the banks of the River of Sorrow that flows with blood and there they are greeted by boatmen who are willing to grant the spirits safe passage across the river if the spirits had led a life that was deemed worthy. I was neither intimidated nor put-off by Vichitra's appearance. I merely shrugged my shoulders and walked on.

For the spirit that has accrued merits by performing acts of kindness and compassion, passage is granted across the river. For the spirit that hasn't, it is left to drown while the remaining flesh on the spirit body is nibbled at continuously. The decayed and decomposed body is torn off in small bits by a multitude of sharp teethed fish that lurk beneath the reddened waters of the river. I felt the intense pain of my flesh being ripped apart. "Repent" said the voice in my head and I did.

The emissaries of Yama then removed the noose and affixed a skewer to my lips. It pierced the upper lip and went right through the lower. A thin cord was tied to the hilt of the skewer which resembled the eye of a needle. I was dragged across the River of Sorrow by Yama's emissaries who took to the air and towed me across by pulling at the cord attached to the upper end of the skewer. The pain was immeasurable. When I reached the other side, I was famished and I once again I fed on the offerings made by my next of kin that appeared like clockwork at the appointed time.

At the start of the seventh month we reached the City of Solitude. Here I was left in peaceful silence, to ponder and reflect on my actions and savor the offerings of food and sweets made by my next of kin. I lamented not on the loss of material wealth nor of earthly possessions.

Having been allowed to contemplate the life that I had led, we departed for the City of Despair, traveling in the air like flighted birds. During the flight I was stung repeatedly by winged insects.

The torments continued for two whole months. At the end of the ninth month we departed for the City of Anguish that was filled with the unnerving noise of thousands of wailing spirits. Spirits that belonged to the faint hearted sank immediately into despair as the loud and audible laments of the lost filled their ears. After spending a whole month in the dismal city, at the end of the tenth month, we departed for the City of Desolation.

At the completion of the eleventh month we journeyed to the City of Respite. Here once again I was able to enjoy the offerings made by my next of kin. After a fortnight the skewer was removed and once again I found the hangman's noose found around my neck.

I was dragged with the noose to the City of Storms. As I approached I saw dark cloud gather and it rained relentlessly without stop. Thunder continuously crashed overhead and I was repeatedly struck by lightning.

By that time a year had passed since my demise and I was no longer dependent on offerings from my next of kin. I was then taken to the City of Fallaway. Here the decomposed remains that had clung like disheveled clothes to my body finally fell away, freeing my soul which was a light no larger than the size of a mortal thumb. Not a single shred of skin remained.

I took to the air with the messengers of Yama, freed from the noose, to the abode of the King of Death, who presided over the City of Death. The City of Yama had four gateways, each facing a separate direction. The southern gateway was allotted to sinful souls. I entered through the northern gate which was reserved for divine entities.

All things alive required some form of sustenance and the soul was very much alive and remained long after the body had been reduced to dust. While the body requires rest and gradually deteriorates with age, the soul remains the same, constant and perpetual, unburdened by the passage of time. The body is fed with food while the soul is fed with good deeds and positive energy that is derived from charitable acts.

Even the humblest of men, those who exist in the lowest strata of society often shunned and ignored by the status quo derive some form of satisfaction from helping others.

When I entered the City of the Dead I was greeted by the doorkeeper, the ever vigilant Dharmadhwaja. The door keeper reported my arrival to Yama's minister in chief, Chitragupta, who tallied the merits of the soul in accordance with its conduct while it was encased in a mortal body. Good deeds that I had performed during my lifetime were weighed against my misdeeds and a synopsis was submitted to Yama.

The King of Death then asked Chitragupta, to elaborate on my misdeeds and the all-knowing Chitragupta, despite knowing the truth, consulted the sons of the creator Brahma, the sravanas, as dictated by custom and tradition.

The sravanas had the ability to travel as fleet as the wind through existence ascending to the highest heavens and descending to the lowest depths, to the heart of the three worlds below and therefore were all knowing and all seeing. They reported all things to Chitragupta, with the utmost discretion, unknown to anyone. Bound at birth to speak only the truth, the all-seeing sravanas, spoke of my virtues and vices to Chitragupta.

To the soul that has lived its life, with truth, honor and kindness, never failing to perform charitable deeds, Yama is benevolent. To the wicked and sinful, Yama dispensed untold misery. Holy and pious people see Yama as a God of noble countenance while the sinful and the wicked see him as a God with dreadful and wrathful features.

Yama, having assured himself of my sins and vices summoned me to his throne room. I did as I was told and as I entered I saw him seated on his buffalo with staff in his right hand longer in length than the height of a full grown man, his eye the burning red of a thousand funeral pyres. He glared at me and when he spoke his voice was as blaring as the sound of a thousand thunders.

I saw him as a god of noble countenance and to me he said "know this, Amesha Spenta". "I deal with all manner of men and women, the rich and the poor, beggars and interlopers, saints and sinners". I remained silent patiently anticipating what was about to come.

I was sent to hell and for the next hundred years I would be confined to this unholy place before I was released and allowed to go on to my next life. The initially million or so precincts were a synch and my soul now freed from the decaying and decomposing body functioned at unprecedented levels. I travelled through the precincts at the rate of knots moving at speeds equivalent to that of light. But even then it took me a hundred years to navigate through all eight million four hundred thousand precincts.

Hell is a prison and the duration of the soul's stay in the prison depends on the crimes that it had committing while it was enshrined or entombed in a mortal body. A person guilty of theft is given an easier sentence than a person guilty of murder. The viler were subjected to more extreme and more intense punishments than the others.

I was never an iniquitous person but yet I had to repay the karmic debt that I had accrued and my stint in hell partly atoned for my misdeeds but that by no means meant that I was totally free. That which was outstanding would still be collected and the debt would be repaid in my next life.

I was subjected to physical torture but by the time of my demise I had become totally devoid of emotion and my senses were numbed. Since the fateful day that I had acquired my sword, I would slowly let my emotions go and gradually in the space of the five years that it would take me to become Amesha Spenta I would be devoid of all emotions. I think I decided the day I plunged a dagger into Chandi's belly that emotions were wasteful. Duty was of paramount importance and in process of fulfilling my obligations all else fell to the wayside.

The blazing inferno that is hell is of immeasurable proportions and it stretched for as far as the eye could see. The drab colors did nothing to liven the place up but it was devoid of the much vaunted screams of pain and suffering that mortals allot to it. If anything the silence was deafening. Maybe the tortured souls were screaming but their screams were inaudible to my ears, I couldn't say. I did not shrink nor cower at the sight of the tormented souls but was repulsed. In time however my revulsion would slowly wane away and I would become more accepting and understanding.

I thought of the numerous people that I had sent to hell and it was only fitting that I reflected on my actions. But then I decided that if the need arose I would do it all again. It was not my intention to orchestrate the demise of thousands if not millions, I can't remember the exact figure; maybe I didn't want to or chose to forget.

The needs of the hour dictated my actions and I was compelled by the need to safeguard our religious teachings and principles. I was certain that the Dark Lord would have done the same. The child of Ahriman like me didn't fear hell.

Each precinct was akin to a separate torture chamber that stretched for hundreds of yoganas in all directions and each chamber applied a different mode of punishment corresponding to the crime that had been committed.

Before the sentence was meted out the soul is once again committed to the mortal body and remains trapped in the mortal physique for the duration of the sentence. If multiple crimes were committed then the soul is sent to multiple chambers. If a simple crime is to be punished it was usually enough to repeatedly sever or strike at the extremity that committed it. It was customary to strike over and over again at the nerve that was responsible for the crime.

For those who were overly dominated by lustful and base desires a thrust is repeatedly made with a sword to the groin. The greedy and the gluttonous are repeatedly struck in the navel. Those who had firmly denied their true emotions and corrupted their leadership with ambition are continually struck in the solar plexus. Prideful thinkers and fools who have used their thoughts to serve baser desires are constantly struck in the heart. People who have misunderstood the higher principles of life are repeatedly beheaded.

The most common punishment for deviant priests was to repeatedly severe the jugular. People who extended their life-force to the detriment of others or even drained others of their life-force were repeatedly struck in the pineal gland. Those who had corrupted their true selves were repeatedly struck above the head.

Those who had orchestrated the death of others by summoning the harbinger of death and pestilence, Pazuzu, were themselves repeatedly subjected to the most torrid illnesses and had the demonic image of Pazuzu hover before their very eyes while they languished wafting from one disease infested body to another.

Those who brought about the death of others through fire without first understanding that to sully the flames of Agni or Athra, for all flames embodied the quality of

Agni or Athra, was a crime of the most heinous nature, were themselves subjected to death by torturous flames and their souls were trapped in a reoccurring flame that never stopped raging. It was discomforting, to say the least, to see the souls calling out for assistance. The tormentor would merely smirk at their woeful cries and continue without giving them any rest or reprieve.

The precincts continued in this manner and those who had completed their sentences were left to wander aimlessly along the corridors of hell until such time as Yama saw it fit to release them from his clutches.

The souls do not forget the time they had spent in hell and the most tortured souls despite having served out their sentences remember the pain that they had been subjected to and when these souls are reborn, it is often in the lower strata of society or in the lowly form of an animal. Guilty souls that are deemed fit to be blessed with a mortal body carry with them the scars that they had acquired in hell and therefore fail to succeed in their new life.

The subconscious mind remembers all things and records every detail. Therefore where possible it is only fitting to live in a manner that fulfills the requirements of Asha, the values behind the resplendent flames of Agni or Athra which are honesty, integrity, equality and justice. Where the body has lived a life devoid of these values, the soul suffers and upon death it is faced with retribution. It is this process of retribution that determines its physical and mental attributes in its next life. If it has sinned little that it owes little and is reborn as a person in a higher station of life or may even attain salvation.

Hell isn't the only destination for the spirits of the dead. Granted that it was the destination for most spirits but below hell is another world called the underworld or the netherworld, the realm of Ereshkigal, the queen of darkness, who lured the most valiant warriors to her palace located in a subterranean cave called Irkalla, the darkest and most desolate place in the underworld. For souls who had visited Irkalla, hell was a breeze.

Ereshkigal invited the most noted warriors, upon death, to feast with her for an eternity in her palace of infamy. These souls after they had completed their sentences in hell were not destined to be reborn. Yama deemed it only prudent to save the world from the destructive forces that swelled within them. Here these valiant warriors drank wine and ate the meat of the beast that resurrected itself at the dawn of each day only to be consumed by the spirits of great warriors* who thronged to the halls of Irkalla at nightfall in the company of the sultry and seductive queen of the underworld. That is as far down as mortal spirits can go.

Below the underworld there is of course the abyss and the angel of death Abaddon is tasked with the duty of keeping the legions of the fallen that were vanquished in the battle before time shackled within the gates of the abyss. Abaddon himself is a somewhat dubious character and in the years that had lapsed since the great battle, when the forces of light confronted the forces of darkness for control of the known world, he had managed to let a demon or two escape. Abaddon is loyal to no one but himself.

---

*   For those who were destined for Irkalla, the soul remained trapped in the spirit that is clothed with the flesh of the warrior moments prior to death

The three worlds of the dead are collectively known as the nether regions and all evil stems from either one or all of these three worlds. No mortal has ventured into all three worlds of the dead, safe but one, me, and as I walk down the corridors of hell, with scenes of torture on all sides, I do so without concern. Death is sometimes a reprieve, a reprieve from the mortal duties that have tormented me endlessly.

Natasha I

Lamunia
1037 NW
Dadgem Garrison

Dear Father,

It is with great regret and it pains my heart no end to inform you that your favorite city in Lamunia, the city where you requested for my mother's hand on a warm summer day along the shores of the River Zohreb, Parsabad, no longer exists. It was razed to the ground and every citadel, home and cornerstone that was once a standing testament to the ingenuity of its vibrant and colorful people was reduced to ashes.

As you well know this was a commission that I accepted with a heavy heart and it was because I was bound by my duty to our sworn liege, the God King, Amesha Spenta. Duty compelled me to accept the burden of leadership when I was content to remain within the secure borders of Mirkash without a need or a care in the world.

Home seems so distant now and being stationed here in the middle of a kingdom that is about to be devastated by war and torn to tatters by ceaseless battles, bloodied by the senseless and often meaningless killings, I am beginning to lose all hope for humanity.

I am overwhelmed by the tide of refugees that continue to flood through like an unending human deluge, people fleeing their homes with their meager possessions or just the plain clothes on their backs. Their individual stories reflect unbearable pain, loss and suffering.

It was a mass exodus triggered by the ten thousand strong invasion, five thousand on foot and five thousand on horseback that crossed the Zohreb on a dark and desolate night. An additional hundred thousand soldiers remain encamped on the other side of the river preparing for what is without doubt a major onslaught.

The encampments include an unknown number of wooden enclosures reinforced with steel and large tapered towers for archers not to mention other battle implements like bricoles*, catapults, cats**, mangonels*** and mantelets****. The wooden enclosures and towers are constructed on wheeled platforms and maneuvered with the help of horses.

What we have seen thus far is only the tip of the iceberg, a minor force which is merely a prelude to the battle to come but even that was enough to send thousands of villagers fleeing. The unexpected incursion took the villagers by surprise and many of them fled with the clothes on their

---

* *A small mortal powered ballistic weapon that hurls small rocks and stones. It is designed to hit groups of foot-soldiers or horsemen.*
** *Wooden structures mounted on wheels and covered with fire-proof materials like animal hides, divots and earth doused with water.*
*** *A siege weapon with a long mast moved with fixed counterweights used to hurl stones.*
**** *Large shields built from wood and wicker that attackers could use to push forward.*

back. The fleeing refuges created a human buffer between the garrison at Dadgem and the enemy.

By the time I assumed command the spate of refugees was well on its way to being unmanageable and unable to stem the tide I ordered my men to assist as much as they could even if it impeded our own progress. I must admit I avoided confronting the enemy whenever permissible to enable our troops to remain fresh in the hope that the invaders would be beleaguered by the onset of winter. I thought it only wise to remain in warmer pastures but I fear that my ploy has not yielded much success and the enemy may soon be at our gates.

The God King has ordered that we take every measure to thwart the progress of the enemy including destroying crops and livestock that cannot be salvaged. It is a distressing task for while I see the military merits of resorting to such unsavory tactics humanity compels me to question his orders. Is the sanctity of our religion so shallow that we need to starve our enemies to death not to mention the villagers that we will eventually leave behind who will no doubt succumb to hunger and other related illnesses?

But I am bound by my oath of fidelity and loyalty and shackled by the chains of gratitude and servitude. My personal convictions have given way to the pressing needs of Hawk's Nest which requires subservient and uncompromising service.

The best we could muster for the refugees was to construct rudimentary shelters from materials that we had on hand or we could forage or salvage including wood, animal skins and pelts. I must admit that this is only a temporary measure for I fear that we may be forced to withdraw further and the wave of refugees that currently stand between us and the enemy may be forced to follow. Therefore I question the value of constructing any form of shelters that are affixed to the land.

We are faced with acute shortages of food and medical supplies and despite my orders to the contrary the men continue to share their rations and their generosity increases my concern. It is foreseeable that if the situation does not improve in the near future, we may be exposed to severe bouts of malnutrition.

Other sicknesses include those them stem from poor hygiene and illnesses induced by a lack of clean drinking water. I have requested for more medical supplies and our allies in the Betan Plateau have thus far been accommodating. As I understand it our supplies are procured from a company that has close ties to Hawk's Nest and thus far they have proved their worth many times over. I must confess that I have yet to meet the proprietors of the enterprise.

We only seek their assistance when it is required. We send a rider out to the nearest stable that doubles up as a station and stocks are replenished within a fortnight to a month depending on the availability and delivered directly to the respective garrisons. I have tried to keep tabs on their riders but it is by no means easy. They must be an organization that employs numerous riders because the faces keep changing all the time.

Their riders travel with pack horses, mules are too slow for the task and often we require these supplies in a hurry. They appear to understand our urgency. It is almost impossible to plan or anticipate the quantities that we need because streams of refugees keep arriving daily and at all hours.

We have however managed to set up checkpoints and employed the services of truth-finders sent to us from Hawk's Nest to discern between real refugees and agents or cohorts of the enemy in disguise. Thus far we have apprehended dozens of spies, all of whom have been put to death by being forced to drink a concoction made from rhododendron honey and hemlock. It brings about a quick demise.

Prior to death the unfortunate recipients experience bouts of hallucinations and temporary spates of madness. This is followed by vomiting spells before the victim is gripped by a state of slowly ascending paralysis. The body then stiffens and the spirit is evicted from the physique.

The irony of it all is that this is the most merciful punishment I can offer or confer to spare those that have been adjudged guilty from facing the wrong end of an executioner's axe. It is safe to say that the guillotines have gone to rust since my arrival.

Amesha Spenta has ordered that all spies be put to an instant death and despite my pleas to try to rehabilitate the offenders beforehand, my petitions have been dismissed by the God King. Maybe he knows something I don't.

I have met him once on an occasion in Mirkash at your court during an impromptu visit when he barged in dressed in the flowing turmeric robes of a monk accompanied by a lovely lady clad in silken red garments whose face beheld the beauty of the ages.

He was tall and lanky and appeared shy with his hair reaching down to his shoulders. He had an odd sword strapped to his back that had a strange hilt affixed to the top decorated by what looked like strands of hair but I could be mistaken. I doubt that the God King would have scalped anyone. If it wasn't for the regal looking lady I would have dismissed him for a wondering monk in search of alms.

The lady as you told me later is the living goddess, a living incarnate who personifies all the positive qualities and aspects of the Brahmatma. She was more dazzling then a thousand diamonds shinning all at once and I was compelled to go down on my knees in reverence as soon as I saw her. She must have read my thoughts because she signaled for me to be still with a slight lift of her hand.

I stood there like a tree rooted to the ground and she walked up to me. I lowered my head as a sign of respect when she approached. She smiled tenderly at the gesture. She referred to me as the girl with the armor of the sun. I smiled. I had almost all but forgotten about my armor of invisibility. She warned me never to give my armor away because as soon as I did I'd be vanquished. "Even if you gave it away child, it won't be of any use to anyone. For the armor to be effective, the recipient must first be blessed by the Sun God himself, as you were when you were born" she said. I remember her words to this very day.

I still remember our daily chants in honor of the Sun God: - "Behold he who Dawn heralds with her rosy fingers and him who the heavenly trumpeters greet with the crow of a rooster. Behold he who rides his golden chariot drawn by his solar steeds that neither stray nor falter. Behold he who shines with the brilliance of a thousand stars and burns with the effulgence of a thousand suns. Behold he who is blanketed by the constellations once the day is done".

"Behold he whose refulgence is witnessed throughout the known world, the live giver who breathes life into all things living and he who inspires warmth into all things breathing - he whose resplendent light never ceases to shine like a beacon in the night".

"He appears beautiful in the horizon sky, the golden disk that signals the beginning of life. When he rises over the horizon the land is filled with mirth and laughter. Let us venerate him whose light extends to all things created and prevails over all that is uncreated".

I can't help but repeat the lines of the sacred hymn though I must admit I can't remember much of him.

The living goddess lifted my chin with her index finger and gently kissed me on the forehead. I felt my body glow when she did so resonating with the brilliance of the sun. She brought my armor to life and it was the first and only time I've felt its radiance in totality.

Of Amesha Spenta himself I can't say much, he looked subdued but his eyes were ablaze with fire so intense that it almost scorched my skin. He looked like a man who was possessed. There was something within him and I felt that it was only the Goddess who kept him within the folds of sanity. He smiled a lovely dimpled smile that was almost impossible to resist but apart from that he appeared silent, cold, distant and withdrawn.

Therefore I was not at all surprised by his order to execute the prisoners. Still it could have been worse I suppose and instead of beheading them he could have ordered them impaled. I petitioned the overlord on the matter and wrote him a compelling letter, clearly indicating my unwillingness to execute anyone. I opted instead to have the captives rehabilitated.

I petitioned that they be given a second chance at life. No doubt they have been led astray by the forces of darkness but there is always hope for the future. The overlord however remained silent and did not answer my first petition. After a month had lapsed, I wrote him a second complaint, more poignant than the first, and almost a month later, close to the beginning of the new moon cycle, I received a reply, directing me to the office of Amesha Spenta.

I was visibly upset at the overly bureaucratic approach that Hawk's Nest adopted and I sent the overlord a formal complaint with my seal on it in addition to sending a letter to the God King requesting that he take immediate action. Finally after my third and fourth attempts I received a letter from Amesha Spenta stating bluntly, for he is not one to mince words, that I could dispose of the prisoners anyway I saw fit. He granted me the authority to do so but he qualified it by saying that the spirit must be separated from the body within three days of the offenders being convicted. Rhododendron honey and hemlock was the most humane means I could think of doing so.

Those that were apprehended were locked away in steel cages and interrogated. The process I am told can be very painful and the warrior priests appeared to be experts at using the manifold instruments of torture. I must thank you for not enrolling me into any of their sects and opting instead to have me tutored and mentored within the confines of our own sect the Order of Dawn. I can't but help repeat a hymn in honor of our loving and nurturing Goddess.

"In the light of the morn the fairest of all Goddesses is born. The daughter of the mitras, the darling of the adityas showers us with brilliant light".

"Let us praise Dawn she who rides her golden chariot drawn by her solar steeds whose luster ushers in the morning sun and dispels all traces of the night. They are but sisters

Dawn and Ratri (night), daughters of the primordial goddess Aditi".

"Praise to her who is most worthy of worship, her beams and her splendor, stretch from the heavens above to the depths of the ocean floor. Praise to the goddess with the golden colored hair who is adorned with gold and silver and garlanded with the glory of the morning".

"Praise to the daughter of the heavens whose radiance dispels all doubts and whose brilliance disperses all fear. Like a valiant archer, like a swift warrior, she banishes any lingering traces of tenebrosity".

"She passes easily through the hills and the meadows while her light sparkles off the white waters of the oceans, glistening and glistering, blinding all that is evil, spreading instantly over vast distances".

"Praise to the Goddess who invokes the spirit of rigor and diligence in the hearts of all men - shedding her light on them as she calls them forth from slumber".

"She brings hither the man who worships glory, power, might, food and vigor. Opulent in her manner she favors us like heroes favor their servants. Dawn who brings oblation and stands prominent on the mountain ridges, she who gives wealth to noble heroes, shine your noble light on us".

Allow me also to praise the Goddess Saraswathy, the giver of knowledge, she who instills wisdom in the hearts of all men. She who is amongst the highest divinities, the goddess of plentitude, with shapes a many - she who is the keeper of wisdom who lights the passageway to eternal glory.

"Let us praise her who is also known as prudence, chastity, temperance, charity, diligence, patience, kindness, humility and intelligence. Praise to the Goddess who stands tall afore all our shrines, whose intensity, strength, power and potency protects all our flock. Praise to her who is abundant in spiritual and intellectual capacity".

Father, we owe the daughters of Aditi our eternal gratitude for without them, despite the radiant armor that crowns my complexion I would be deprived of the ability to defend my values in the presence of the God King. I choose to follow but I do not choose to follow blindly.

Amesha Spenta entrusted me with the defenses of Lamunia and in furtherance of his decision to hasten my appointment, as you well know my nomination was not without objection, I was furnished with reports from the intelligence committee.

Through these reports I have been able to garner some facts about my opponent who leads a hundred and ten thousand strong army against us. His name is Azag son of Grog, a former King of Kish, a territory in the Central Kingdoms. He was resurrected from the underworld by Ahriman and ransomed from the keeper of the death, Ereshkigal. He has brazenly overwhelmed the Dashian forces that, in truth, have done little to repel the enemy who have so ruthlessly infringed on their sovereignty.

Instead they have meekly accepted a truce thereby allowing Azag's men free and unhindered passage through Dashia. Azag is now camped along the banks of the River Zohreb and plans to cross the river to the mouth of the Reasi Valley using rafts and makeshift floats. The valley is covered on both sides by thick forests. The God King has forbidden any incursion into the forest on the western slopes of the Reasi for reasons best known only to him and Hawk's Nest.

Azag has chosen to use the Reasi Valley to secure a passage into Lamunian territories via Kesh which is located at the southern tip of the valley because it is the only feasible route that permits infantry mobility through to Kesh. The forests stretch for about a hundred yoganas to the west and to east of the border and to go further east would take him closer to Hawk's Nest and more formidable opposition.

Dashia is a nation built on a plateau between the Quest Mountains and the Darya River. It was an ailing kingdom that was on the verge of collapse prior to the invasion. Once an important trading route that linked the east to the Central Kingdoms it had declined over time but remained an important artistic and religious stronghold. Because of its historic and religious significance Amesha Spenta has declared it a buffer state and we are prohibited from launching a counter offensive into or from Dashia.

The God King has sent able lieutenants to assist me with the defenses of Lamunia. Our troop strength in Lamunia number in total one hundred and seventy four thousand men and they comprise of the First Corps, the cream of the crop, made up of knights from the Emerald Order who are directly under my command. We are thirty three thousand five hundred strong.

We are supported by twenty thousand battle hardened veterans from the Second Corps under the command of Captain Nazafarin. Both the First and Second Corps are stationed at the garrison in Dadgem.

Almost ten yoganas to the east is the Garrison at Pulwara staffed by troops from the Third and Fourth Corps with a troop strength of forty seven thousand men under the command of Captain Farazmon and Captain Masoud. They are stationed within and around a walled fortress.

The fortress at Pulwara is called the Masada Fort. It was construed during the time of the Grand Empire. It is often referred to as the strongest of all fortresses and was originally erected during the reign of the Empress Amireh, the third ruler and the most exulted monarch of the Grand Empire. The fort in located at the summit of a hill. During the reign of Ozra, the most influential of all Lamunian Kings, who was born approximately three centuries after the death of the Empress, it was expanded to four times its original size and buttressed by an addition set of outer walls.

The walls of the fortress are approximately twelve cubits high and eight cubits thick and include large towers. Each tower has a separate passage way leading to the interior of the castle. Ozra built a system of large cisterns to collect rainwater to ensure that there was ample supply of water all year round. The fort is unique and there is none other like it in Lamunia or the surrounding kingdoms.

Ozra also built storehouses for food and wine which he kept fully stocked. On the northwest he built a palace which included among other things a bathhouse. At the extreme north of the summit was a three tiered private villa built for Ozra's personal use which has now been acquisitioned by Captain Masoud, the older or the two captains. Farazmon was left to occupy the lesser quarters that were initially reserved for Ozra's retinue, not that he particularly minds the subtle affront.

He is a career minded military officer with a preference for more down to earth accommodations. Masoud on the other hand, who was born into a family of some means, insisted where possible on a plush lifestyle. In spite of his rather aloof outward appearance, it must be said that he has repeatedly managed to come up with level headed solutions.

They are quite the pair Farazmon and Masoud and despite the constant bickering that is antecedent to all their campaigns and has become somewhat of a customary prerequisite, they have managed to thrash things out between them and often come up with viable solutions or wining options. Amesha Spenta has perfect confidence in their abilities and has left them at my disposal.

The Third and Fourth Corps are reinforced by the Fifth and Sixth corps who are located approximately a hundred miles to the south of Masada in the district of Anantnag and comprise of approximately twenty five thousand men under the command of Captains Shahnameh and Sassaniand and included among others local reserves and mercenaries.

The respective captains are assigned with the task of bringing their troops up to speed and I have kept them away from the frontline as much as possible to give them time to train their troops and hone in on their skills. Their effectiveness against Azag's army is questionable but we suffer from an acute shortage of manpower and given the superior battle skills that the invaders possess we are left without choice.

Just to the rear of the troops in Masada, approximately ten yoganas south, in Shupiyan, there are eight thousand five hundred men from the Seventh Corps or the Engineering Corps and they are tasked with building catapults and other siege engines to assist with the defenses of Lamunia. Trees were felled and rocks were gathered and sometimes covered with tar, in readiness to be set alight and loaded onto steel buckets before being flung at the enemy from a distance. The improvisations will allow us to inflict as much damage as possible on the enemy.

They are led by Captain Golnaz and worked alongside men and women from the Eight Corps a majority of whom were skilled archers with longbows who remained hidden in shrubs, bushes and trees, constantly on the lookout for intruders. The orders from their leader Captain Azardokth was to shoot at sight and to take no prisoners. She has in total nine thousand archers at her disposal who could fire an arrow from a bow with deadly precision.

Flanking the First and Second Corps in the west was the Ninth Corps led by Captain Irdeh. They were skilled horsemen whose armor was made from a metallic silver compound, forged specially for them and equipped with lances and bows.

The lances or spears that they wielded was of unusual thickness and length and it was used with such skill that it often had enough impetus to pierce through two men in a single thrust. The bows that they carried were powerful and made of a rare composite. Its arrows shot with swiftness, strength, and precision and were capable of penetrating the toughest armor. They numbered in total seven thousand five hundred men and women who were camped on high ground to ensure that the momentum was always on their side.

The backbone of the army comprised of twenty three thousand five hundred imperial guards from Mirkash our own men who I brought with me. As you well know they are veterans of countless battles who excelled at horsemanship and were equally adept with the sword. They are under the command of Captain Zavareh and are stationed on the Lamunian side of the Lamunian-Amestrian border.

We still have troops who are under-skilled and this coupled with the fact that we are as yet unable to stem the tide of refugees, many of whom brought with them sordid tales of houses and farms being set alight under the cover of darkness by rampaging marauders and our inability to estimate the size of enemy reinforcements sets us at a disadvantage. All we know is that the Dark Lord has a vast arny at his disposal.

I know that in the infinite love and care that you have for me, your tender heart might be tempted to needlessly worry. Let me assure you, dear father that I am well, safe and secure in the company of the men and women I command.

I will write again soon. Until then please do take care and send my love to mother.

Love Always
Natasha

Natasha II

Captain Golnaz busied herself with the task of overseeing the duties that were assigned to her team. In addition to the regular members of the Seventh Corps, the engineering grounds where she and her team worked were also staffed by miners, sappers, carpenters and volunteers who were more than eager to give her a hand. She was tasked with building mechanical weapons that were powered by bows or taut ropes that projected shots at high velocities and propelled missiles over great distances or catapults for short.

The range varied on the construction and the design of the builders or the engineers. To be most effective the catapults had to be lodged on higher ground so that the missiles could travel further and come crashing down harder. The surfaces of the rocks that were to be loaded on to the buckets or slings were first chiseled to smoothen out the rough edges so that they would eventually (once covered with tar or other combustibles and set alight) roll down the hill and inflict as much damage as possible. It was foreseeable that there might be civilian casualties but the God King had insisted that they retaliate as soon as possible despite the likelihood of incurring non-military fatalities.

Golnaz improvised as much as she could to build the perfect weapon. She experimented with vines, sinews and ropes but these materials lost their elasticity in a comparatively short time and if continued pressure was applied they had to be replaced at short intervals. Therefore she had to have a team constantly on standby to make the necessary adjustments.

The formation of the arm of the catapult was another conundrum. The arm had to be able to endure and sustain great strain. The arms of large catapults are composed of spars of wood and bound by broad strips of raw hide.

If the arm that held the sling was too thin, it would snap. A thick arm would certainly be more durable but that would add weight to the mechanism. Undue weight prevented the arm from acting with the speeds required to casting the projectile with good effect. A heavy and ponderous arm of solid wood cannot rival in lightness and effectiveness to a composite arm made of wood, sinew and hide.

It presented Golnaz with a quandary of varying proportions. The former was inert and slow in its action of slinging a stone while the latter was in comparison as quick and as lively as a steel spring.

The next question that popped into the mind of the diligent engineer was the range. The bigger the catapult or the trebuchet (larger catapults were called trebuchets) the farther the range or the longer the distance that the stone or boulder could travel. However larger engines present additional problems principally stealth and mobility. Both factors became especially relevant under the present circumstances in lieu of the fact that the catapults had to be transported through territories presumably teeming with the enemy.

Golnaz decided that stealth was not a conceivable possibility or eventuality and chose instead to channel her energies into constructing a mechanism with greater range and deeper penetration. The established principles of warfare dictated that any mechanism built in anticipation or in furtherance of battle must ideally be able to inflict maximum damage while the side operating the mechanisms sustained minimum loss. The obvious solution was to crush the enemy under a pile of rocks or boulders.

The catapults had to be mounted on wheels to precipitate or accelerate mobility. The transition from one location to another had to be done under the cover of darkness to facilitate stealth. Golnaz doubted stealth was a factor that she could comply with given the size of the apparatus that she had in mind. The stream of people that moved southwards because of the invasion however thinned during the night and that would facilitate mobility and allow the catapults to move faster.

The catapults had to be brought into position and the only viable solution that Golnaz could come up with was for Azardokth, who was charged with getting the catapults to the battle front, to fight her way through.

Archers with the advantage of being stationed on high grounds with the additional advantage of longbows, positioned at distances of twenty paces from each should also be deployed to enable the safe manipulation of the siege engines. Ideally the catapults should be positioned within a defensive perimeter of walled men and shielded where possible with mantelets.

The balista was required to send its missile clear over the heads of those within the defensive perimeter and any other men or women who might be wondering close to the scene. Therefore the engines must have a range of eight hundred to a thousand or so cubits to be as effective and as destructive as they undoubtedly could be. It also meant that the catapults had to be dragged close enough to the edge of the interlocking spurs or the cliffs that overlooked the Zohreb to do the damage that was intended.

In order to increase the effectiveness of the catapults it was decided that a sling made of either rope or leather should be fitted to the arm. The sling of the arm increased its reach by at least one third. In addition to that it was much lighter and recoiled at far greater speeds than an extended arm.

The length of the arm is of some relevance because the longer the arm of the catapult, the longer was its sweep through the air and thus the farther it will cast its projectile provided of course it was not of undue weight.

The firing mechanism is then cocked by setting a round stone to the sling and four soldiers on each side of the engine wind the arm down until it is almost level to the ground. When the arm is released the stone is hurled from its sling and comes crashing down on the other side.

The enemy troops once they had crossed the river on large wooden rafts clambered on to its shores and had to negotiate a valley with interlocking spurs that was covered by steep slopes on both sides before reaching open ground. The hills were ideal for positioning the catapults but it was a matter of getting the siege engines close enough to do the desired damage. It wouldn't be easy by any means and Azag foresee-ably would have had the hills and valleys close to the banks of the Zohreb blanketed with soldiers.

According to reports the men were put on a forced march as soon as they had crossed. The cold nights caused immeasurable delays and the soldiers could be visibly seen huddled together around campfires trying desperately to keep the chill at bay. The horses fared no better and many had thinned during the journey to Lamunia. The men tired from over exertion and privation were disposed to sicknesses as they trundled through the valley. The forced marches continued during the day and the soldiers marched through clouds of sand and dust that were caused by trampling boots, a factor that further contributed to bodily illnesses.

Treatment or the hope of treatment was thus far only an illusion that never materialized. The greater part of the army fought in vain against succumbing to mortal frailties and there was a shortage of all essential supplies. There were no barriers to prevent the spread of disease and many suffered from malnutrition and dehydration. It was apparent that the results of the hardships would soon reach its apex or its climax.

Some of the foot-soldiers had knapsacks on their backs in which they could stock food or water in rudimentary containers including whatever they could pick or plunder along the way.

These men fared better than those that marched without backpacks and were forced to carry whatever they could find in their arms or on their bodies. Others with less stronger constitutions grew more melancholy by the day and would eventually succumb to taking their own lives and hence commit the greatest sin from which there was no reprieve or restitution. Their bodies would be discarded as food for scavenging animals.

Noticing the drop in morale and wanting to prevent further desertion and abandonment of his men from their posts, Captain Niaz, one of the nine commanders under

Azag, who was charged with the preliminary crossing, ordered a halt on the last day before the birth of the new moon.

They rested for the day and on the following night, the night of the full moon, Niaz decided to calcify the will and resolve of his men by invoking the dark gods. It was a black rite strengthened by the negative aspects of the Brahmatma.

The soldiers were ordered to gather in groups and each group was assigned a priest to invoke the powers of darkness. "In the name of Ahriman, the ruler of material pleasures and all things sweet and savored, he who personifies in men an image in his own likeness, I implore the forces of evil that constantly strive to safeguard the divisions of all material pleasures, to bestow their infernal and accursed power on us. May the gates of the three worlds that constitute the nether realms, hell, the underworld and the abyss be opened and may the spirits and demons that are shackled within come forth to greet their brothers and sisters".

The priests continued in unison .... "Hear me o' dark gods, we have forged a thousand alliances and fought a thousand battles. Together we have filled the waterways with the blood of animals, mortals and celestials. We raided, pillaged, looted and enslaved, in unison, as one. We mocked the power of righteousness and heralded the glory of darkness. We fueled the cremation fires with the carcasses of men and we left behind enough meat for vultures to feast on for a hundred years. Come now my brethren join us once again in our search for fame and glory".

The priests then handed around glass beakers filled with a thick red liquid, blood collected from the cut open veins of prisoners and handed them around. Each member of the congregation took a sip of the elixir of life and within minutes went into a stupor.

Drummers started beating on their drums and soon the soldiers began dancing. The beat was slow to start with but increased in tempo as the night got longer.

During the rite the dancers went into a trance and were metaphysically transported to a place that they called the happy killing grounds and there in the company of dead ancestors or other spirits they went into a killing frenzy. These dancers acquired strengths many times that of their normal selves and were able to tear their enemies asunder with their bare hands.

Neither arrow, club nor sword could faze them and they went on a delusional rampage. They danced on unfazed or unhindered by any of the events that transpired. To any onlooker the dancers appeared to be acting strangely. They shook and they trembled violently, some fainted while others stood rigidly rooted to the ground for hours and wondered about in a daze until their bodies tired and sagged to the ground.

The dance was repeated for five continuous nights following the same ritual and in that time the dancers grew leaner and consumed considerably less food but exerted themselves for the duration of the rite. During the transition from one stage to another from the trance state to normality and back, some of the men lost they capacity to reason and upon their return some of them started acting like deranged men.

During their spree in the happy killing grounds those who spoke to the spirits that they encountered established a telepathic link with the spirits and even when they returned to some semblance of normality the link remained open and many succumbed to spirit possession.

The malicious spirits once they had gained the ability to communicate with the men were at liberty to enter their bodies. This was made evident by a sudden dilation of the pupils, unnatural changes to their features or the manner in which they carried themselves including abnormal changes to the voice.

Normal speech would give way to profanities and the men who were possessed developed a sudden craving for raw meat or blood. They would further develop the compulsion to kill, injure or maim other men and animals. It was impossible for the men to restrain themselves from doing so and they were a danger even to themselves.

Preventing those that suffered from acute possession from causing death or injury to themselves was a tiresome burden because their strengths increased many times that of their normal capacity or capability and Niaz did not labor under any misconceptions. No doubt a negligible portion of his men would succumbed to death by their own hands but those that remained more than made up for it in sheer ferocity.

The victims no longer had a need to clean or wash and their personal hygienic conditions and or that of their surroundings deteriorated considerably. The sole objective of the men now was to kill and do as much damage as possible. Their new yearnings suited Niaz well because his men would not be distracted by the needless and often wasteful desire to clean up or crave the normal amenities that they lacked. "Let them be madmen" he decided for that is what the needs of the hour dictated and required.

These men were now instruments of malicious spirits that needed to feed and the most potent form of nourishment for these spirits was the blood of mortals. They occupied physique was no longer subjected to mortal cravings but to spirit cravings.

Niaz took matters a step further and encouraged his men to go on bloodthirsty rampages that he would willingly initiate. Little groups of men would run amok for days and the spree would continue until such time as they were killed or the mortal body could not sustain the demonic cravings any longer and succumbed first to madness then to death. The deranged men unleashed hell on the villagers. Having lost the ability to reason between the army that opposed them and innocent villagers the men killed indiscriminately.

Niaz cared little for the safety or the wellbeing of the men under him. He was given command not for his wit or his ability to lead but for his sheer savagery and his ability to cause unmitigated damage. Niaz intended to drive the possessed men into a killing frenzy and it didn't matter to him if they died in the process. Many would not return but that was a foregone conclusion. His orders were to simply crush the enemy by any means possible and he intended to do just that.

Natasha III

Captain Azardokht's team mobilized round about midnight the first day of the month on a route that will take them through Dadgem where there will be met by a contingent of Emerald Knights who will then escort them as they plodded north to Kesh and from then on they were to make their way to the forested hills east of the Reasi Valley along forest tracks.

The first leg of the journey was relatively smooth and despite the four siege engines to the rear, dragged by horses, the archers, foot-soldiers and men chosen to work the catapults made good progress. It was the first leg of their journey and the trip thus far had progressed smoothly partly because they travelled through friendly territory.

The tracks were typical of the dirt tracks of Lamunia hardened by the frost of nightfall but easy enough to trample on. They arrived at Dadgem within a fortnight of leaving Shupiyan and were greeted at the border by the Emerald Guards. Captain Azardokht retained overall command. Her men cut across Dadgem in no time heading northeast and soon arrived at Kesh.

They decided to make the journey under the cover of darkness, braving the cold conditions to avoid the barrage of fleeing men, women and children. On the third day out of

Kesh they stumbled onto stray groups of men, deserters no doubt, foraging for food and supplies along the countryside. They looked tired, worn out and demoralized and didn't appear to take any notice of the captain's arrival. The astute Azardokht had her men quietly take up positions, ready to fire if called upon but the splintered and disheveled group dressed in fatigues that were weathered and dirty with clear evidence of wear and tear looked unperturbed and had their attentions diverted elsewhere.

Azardokht was a shrewd woman. Her blonde hair, which was whitened by continued exposure to the sun sat neatly on her shoulders while her shimmering blue eyes took into account every minor detail. Her features were sharp, hawkish and her tall, lean frame allowed her to handle a bow with a dexterity that rivaled Karmina the noted archeress from Hawk's Nest.

The scavenging soldiers presented her with a problem that most commanders would rather avoid. The men looked harmless and while she felt a tinge a of sympathy sweep through her body, she questioned the merits of leaving behind an enemy in the rear. The decision to be merciful may come back to haunt her. Prudence dictated that she left behind no loose ends. Bearing this in mind she gave the order to kill. It looked more like an execution that a fight because many of the scavengers did not have the will to resist and death may have been an escape from a fate much worse. Maybe they were lucky and despite having come to an uninspiring end their souls may still remain untainted and salvation may not be beyond their grasp.

She prayed that the skies would be filled with vultures the following morning and that the vultures filled their bellies with the remains of the dead men to keep the essence of Druj from defiling and contaminating the earth.

Death was swift and merciful. The captain watched her men clinically finish off the enemy and as the arrows stuck their bodies, she caught sight of something that slightly unhinged her. She was unnerved by what she saw. The eyes of the soldiers were diluted, like they were under the influence of some type of intoxicant that had deprived them, temporarily at least, of their sanity. Worse yet was the color of their eyes. The normal white had been displaced by a daunting red.

She paused and reasoned. It was obvious that she wasn't dealing with normal men. She suspected that many of the men were under the influence of lesser spirits. It was relatively easy to gauge the strength of the spirits that possessed the bodies by the actions of the men and these men were under the influence of spirits that did not have the will to resist but were content to feed on whatever they could salvage.

She instantly summoned a rider and sent a message to Natasha. The princess would no doubt be keen on hearing what she had uncovered as would the office of Amesha Spenta. To some extent she felt relieved. The burden of killing was lifted from her shoulders for the men were already death and by bringing about the demise of their physical bodies, she was relieving the tormented soul and hastening its journey to the next life.

The longer the possessed body remained in the mortal plane the more prolonged was the journey on the road to redemption and the slimmer the chances of the soul finding salvation or reaching the hereafter. It was highly likely that the tainted soul would be subjected to rebirth and encased in the body of a lowly animal.

They continued to make steady progress for about a week, travelling only at nights, unaffected by the chilly conditions, partly due to the steady pace they were moving at. The next minor skirmish occurred at a clearing beside a farmhouse. From all appearances it appeared to be a farmstead whose occupants had been forced to flee because of the current conflict. The scouts spotted a herd of unsaddled horses and close by there were men sitting around a campfire having a meal. They looked much different to the scavengers that traversed aimlessly along the countryside separated and scattered from their units. These men wore good quality armor which had the outward appearance of having been forged by quality blacksmiths. It was obvious to the captain that she was dealing with a more elite group of soldiers.

She studied them from afar, hidden by a clump of trees, astride her chestnut stallion. It was a tossup between having them ridden down by the knights or having her archers expediently finish the job from a safe distance. She ordered the knights into position but decided to deploy her archers instead. They knights were readied just in case there were more men inside the house. The scouts had taken the precaution of counting the number of horses that were left to graze freely close to the farmhouse and it tallied with the men around the campfire.

Arrows were effective anyway from eighty to one hundred and twenty cubits depending on the prowess of the archer. To the untrained eye the crossbow might have been more advantageous in the present situation but there were a few factors that came into play and the choice of weapons was crucial to the success of their mission.

The crossbow had a slight efficiency advantage over the conventional bow. It had an exceptional draw force that was a result of an ability to hold tension for an extended time period. The arrow however covered more feet per second when fired from a conventional bow but the crossbow had the additional advantage of allowing archers to use a shooting rail which allowed for greater accuracy.

The crossbow was not without its disadvantages. It was normally bigger and heavier than a conventional bow and presented the archer with the challenge of carrying it or lugging it around which became cumbersome especially on lengthy journeys along rugged terrains or forested tracks.

The crossbow is also noisier than the conventional bow. The tremendous draw forces caused vibrations and vibrations translated to noise that may be audible to keen ears especially those belonging to animals. Deer for example have an exceptionally fast reaction time and in most instances the quieter the hunter the more successful he would be.

In addition to that it takes an enormous amount of energy to draw a crossbow and it is not ideal for those without the requisite upper body strength. Conventional bows made from different composites were light, easy to draw on and could be crafted to suit the archer's needs or tailored to meet his or her physical requirements. Given the above considerations Azardokht had decided to dispense with the crossbow and chose instead to equip her men with conventional bows.

The captain could bring down an enemy from distances exceeding one hundred and twenty cubits but she like Karmina was an exception. Eighty cubits was a safe bet for a normal man or woman.

Her archers had to cautiously inch closer without making a sound and they had to make sure that they remained downwind or else the horses might pick up their scent and they would get uneasy and restless in which case they would start to mill around, throw their heads about and stomp their feet on the ground which would alert the soldiers.

Azardokht's men had to creep as silently forward as possible and a good ten minutes ticked by before they were in position. At the first whizz of the arrow the soldiers leapt to their feet and reached for the swords that was strapped to their side but the archers reloaded their bows swiftly and released a second volley of arrows without giving them a chance to recover or retaliate.

From then on matters got lively and the knights and archers were constantly called into action. They had to shoot, cleave and hack their way through and despite staying away from well-traveled routes and opting to use forest tracks, the clashes did not diminish and Azardokth had to request for reinforcements which arrived in the form of archers and foot-soldiers in no time.

Rural Lamunia was densely forested and covered with tall trees that seemed to rise upwards forever. The thick canopy of green prevented the sunlight from filtering through to the ground and therefore the forest floors were not covered with dense undergrowth. This made smooth passage possible but it was unsuited to cavalry battles or battles on horseback. Riders had to be on the lookout for branches that stuck out from nowhere to avoid riding into them and being flung off their horses.

Riders stayed on the dirt tracks while many of the archers and foot-soldiers preferred to make their way through the woods that not only provided them with cover but also high vantage points from which they could fire their arrows at greater velocity. It was a terrain ideally suited to archers but the worry ahead was that they had to find suitable clearings to position their catapults. The tall trees made it impossible for the siege engines to be of much use at present.

In addition to getting the catapults into position Azardokht also had to plot a route that was defendable to permit reinforcements to arrive and to enable supplies to be delivered in a timely manner. As she ventured closer to the Zohreb the size of her troops began to diminish due to fatalities incurred during repeated skirmishes. She had to leave behind groups of men and women to safeguard the passage that they had carved out or else she was at risk of being cut off or isolated.

The route was not as heavily infiltrated as they had expected or anticipated. A month into what was developing to be a slow and tedious journey forward the contingent of men and women under the captain's command were testament to the morbid sights of war. Instead of witnessing courage, valor, comradeship and all the other aspects of war that inspired men to be warriors, they witnessed hunger, disease and pestilence that robbed men and women of their lives and their livelihoods.

As they progressed the scouts brought back reports of masses of soldiers camped on the shores of the Zohreb and the march along the valley was well underway. It was imperative that the valley be defended under all circumstances.

They had taken into account of the possibility of the enemy, crossing the Zohreb and landing on the more densely forested areas. However if that were true the forests that they were navigating through would be teeming with enemy soldiers but thus far that had not happened. The men that they had encountered were at best deserters foraging for food or advanced parties that were on routine scouting or raiding missions.

Azardokth was beginning to get a clearer picture of the situation. Azag like a wise general had decided to keep his troops intact with the intention of assembling his men on the shores off the Zohreb and then making a clear incisive sweep along the valley all the way through to Kesh. His plan was simply to muscle his way through. What they had encountered so far was only the first wave and the biggest battle would be fought on the Lamunian side of the Zohreb to secure the valley. It was essential for both sides to hold their positions.

She had a rider take her findings to Natasha and she received a response within a fortnight. The princess agreed with her and ordered her to defend the valley at all cost. To this effect she sent in more troops, comprising mainly of foot-soldiers and archers to aid with the defense of the valley. She also sent workmen to help with the clearing of trees and assist with other tasks that needed to be done in an encampment, including creating defensive perimeters.

Natasha IV

The Valley of Reasi was between half a yogana to a yogana in width with interloping hilly forests on both sides. Despite outward appearances Azag had limited amphibious resources and it was difficult for him to contemplate simultaneous landings on more than one front on the densely forested Kupwara coast. His objective was to break through the Lamunian defenses and reach Kesh approximately four yoganas inland from where he could launch an offensive into Dadgem to the southwest of Kesh and the fort at Pulwara to the southeast of Kesh and then onto Lamunia proper. To this effect he ordered Captain Niaz to cross the Zohreb and cleave a passage southward. The outcome of the battle he decided would be determined by strong resolute action.

Azag was a ruthless commander and his troops were hard pushed and hard pressed. The Lamunian defenses thanks to Golnaz's improvisations and Azardokht's astuteness had delayed their advance by entrenching themselves in fortified areas. Azardokht had managed to secure a passage to the cliffs that overlooked the Zohreb and had managed to, in a short space of time, clear the trees at the edge of the slopes to position the catapults.

The slopes were by no means easy to assail and she had sufficient men, temporarily at least with more on the way, to help her defend her position. Azag's men were repeatedly pounded by a barrage of rocks and shrapnel. The defenders had also managed to dig a series of trenches to protect the siege engines and to negate the possibility of the enemy orchestrating a successful assault. Niaz's men thus far had only managed to get themselves killed in their attempts to dismantle the catapults and scaling the steep slopes had proved futile. The casualties were so severe that Azag even contemplated ignoring the catapults and absorbing the loss.

Azardokth managed the catapults well, using two catapults at time to fill different sections of the valley with rocks, stones, gravel, sharp wooden spikes and anything else that would hinder or thwart the enemy progress. These included rocks smothered with tar and set alight. Golnaz's innovations were doing a smashing job and caused severe damage to the enemy.

Repeated firing however caused the catapults to lose their elasticity at a fairly rapid rate and the ropes, vines and sinew that determined the elasticity of the catapults had to be replaced at frequent intervals. The men however were more than up to the task and the overall morale among them was good.

Rocks were another conundrum because they were not always readily available and while she waited for the missiles to be replenished, something that occurred at fairly regular intervals, the workers and volunteers were tasked with leveling trees and carving out small sharp spikes that could be hurled from the metal buckets of the catapults.

A majority of Niaz's men suffered at the very least from minor injuries and abrasions. Their captain was infuriated. Thus far his men hadn't managed to make as much as a dent and even when they managed to scale the cliffs that lodged the catapults which was by no means an easy feat they still had to overcome a battery of skilled archers.

Unaware of Azag's amphibious limitations and fearing a landing on the forested fronts along the coast of the Zohreb, Natasha had her men watch every cubit of the eastern sector of the Reasi Valley. She could do little about the western sector because she was under strict orders to stay clear of it. Prudence however dictated that she leave nothing to chance and she had Captain Nazafarin and her Emerald Knights scour every possible opening along the mouth of the forest for signs of infiltration.

Despite the repeated firing the rafts kept coming. Summer was fast giving way and autumn was gaining ground but there wasn't the slightest hint that the enemy was slowing down. If anything Azag quickened or hastened the pace and Natasha had to repeatedly reinforce her troops between Kesh and Azardokth's catapults to defend the route. Fatigue was a major concern on both sides.

Much of the fighting was confined to the valley and after a month of relentless fighting Azag's men hadn't made much progress and found themselves often pinned to the ground by falling rocks, stones and gravel. The team of workers that accompanied Azardokth had also managed to construct makeshift bricoles that were ideal for launching hot coal that was mined further east.

They had been resourceful enough to secure an ample supply of coal, courtesy of their friends in the Betan Peninsula, who had fortuitously acquired mounds of coal (one mound is equivalent to the weight of a normal man). Small rocks of coal, the size of man's fist, were first heated in a furnace and loaded on to metal buckets before being hurled at the invaders. The small smoldering rocks that fragmented into smaller bits when they came in contact with the body not only stung but often set clothes and other combustible materials alight in addition to sending horses into a frenzy.

Niaz had managed to work out that it was impossible to repeatedly shell his men and he waited for the firing to stop, which occurred at fairly frequent intervals, before he ordered his men to resume their march forward. As soon as the firing recommenced his men would immediately seek shelter.

From Azardokht's perspective she could not continue firing repeatedly. As much as she would have liked to, she just didn't have the resources to do so. She wished that she had a hundred catapults on hand but at present the best she could muster was four.

It was at about this time that scouts started to bring in word of armored vehicles. From the descriptions that were given, Azardokth gathered that the vehicles resembled enclosed carriages with hollowed insides that seated between four to six men. The wooden exterior was reinforced with thin sheets of metal.

The driver was easy prey as were the horses that pulled the carriages and would succumb to arrows fired from bows. But those within the enclosed compartments were not that easy to kill and they were armed and trained to retaliate. There were sight windows on all four sides from which archers could fire arrows from conventional bows or crossbows. With the exception of dropping a boulder on the carriages or setting the fortified enclosure alight, the hybrid mantelets were impossible to neutralize. Golnaz swore profusely when she heard the news and kicked herself for not thinking of something similar.

The battle swung back and forth and heavy resistance stalled Azag's advance. Adding to his woes was news that the battle further south was not going as planned. A division of the Second Corps launched deliberate and calculated counter attacks to wear his men down and the trickle of men that had managed to fight their way through to the other end after braving the narrow interlocking spurs that divided the eastern forest from the western forest and trudging up a steep harrowing hill were easy pickings for the horse lancers who swooped down at the them from their concealed locations. Repeated attacks delayed any further advances and often negated any gains that they had made.

Azag's men however managed to form a thin defensive line that stretched from the mouth of the valley to Kesh but the Second Corps were a thorn in their flesh. Similarly, Natasha's men held another line that stretched to the slopes that bordered the Zohreb on the eastern sector of the valley. The shortest distance between both lines was half a yogana and there was still enough space between both lines to stop the men from coming to a face to face confrontation.

The horse lancers who attacked from the west of Kesh skillfully probed the gaps in Azag's line, exploiting weaknesses often caused by a lack of communication between the troops and their somewhat deranged captain to their advantage.

Azag's response was swift and decisive. He moved his tactical headquarters, to the west and ordered landings on the coast of the western slopes of the valley where the rafts were out of catapult reach.

He intended for his men upon landing to scale the cliffs on the western sector of the Reasi which was undefended unlike the eastern beachhead. Within days without the adversity of swirling currents, a new batch of men under the command of Captain Khasham had managed to amass a landing on the western shore and had successfully scaled its slopes, ready to brave the daunting forest that lay ahead. The men were on foot and lightly armored, factors which allowed them to expediently scale the cliffs. Khasham orders were to negotiate the forest and position his men on Natasha's flank and maneuver his way to Kesh.

The western forest of the Reasi Valley was rumored to be inhabited not only by wild animals but also by devils with pointed ears who would not hesitate to prey on any mortal that intruded into their forest. Azag hoped that Khasham had remained faithful in his prayers to Ahriman. The devils in question were normally referred to by those well versed in elven lore as dark elves and they were perverse and twisted beyond mortal comprehension.

Azag had full knowledge of this minor detail before he sent Khasham on his mission but he hoped that Khasham and his men would be spared by virtue of their loyalty and fidelity to the forces of darkness. It was a calculated risk that he had to take. He wasn't sure if his counterpart on the Lamunian side was aware of the little fact and if she wasn't maybe he could entice her to send her men into the forest. He was certain that the dark elves wouldn't look favorably on them at all.

Dark elves were creatures that despised the sun and resided in deep subterranean caves located below the forest surface untouched by the rays of the sun. They were hideous creatures, slightly shorter than normal elves or light elves that ventured out of their caves at nightfall to prey on their victims, haunting and taunting them in their dreams. Dark elves were active only from the time the sun set to dawn.

They were normally around four cubits in height though some can grow up to four and a half cubits and were often naked to the waist and below their knees. Their bodies were filled with clumps of mangled and matted hair and their teeth were sharp and spiked. They were the exact opposite to their arch rivals the light elves.

Dark elves like the succubus preyed on their victim's dreams. But while the succubus does not reveal her physical presence, dark elves sit on their victim's bodies during the invasion and the victims can often feel the weight of the dark elf on their bodies while their dreams were being intruded.

Unlike the succubus that haunts her victims with dreams of erotic pleasures, slowly draining the blood from their veins in the process, dark elves invaded the dreams of their victims with nightmares so daunting that the victims hearts may stop beating during the course of the dream. Horrific blood rites are trademarks of dreams imposed on by dark elves.

Dark elves cannot be exposed to the light of the sun and the radiant rays of Shamash if it touched the skin of a dark elf turned the deviant creatures to stone.

Azag was not without his share of difficulties. His troops were facing an entrenched defense aided by aerial missiles and flying projectiles while they grappled with food and medical shortages. The catapults had him in a dilemma and he had to choose between pressing on with the offensive or waiting until his men had constructed more floatables to help them with the crossing.

The torrid weather made matters increasingly difficult. Some of the defending units splintered as reinforcements continued to pour in and begun operating like partisans, using guerilla tactics and deploying swift counter attacks picking on lone outfits and stragglers before disappearing into the cover of the eastern forest. The terrain was ideally suited to this type of warfare, given the dense forest cover and without adequate mobility he was hard pressed to give chase. Despite the stiffening resistance and well organized counter attacks, Azag's men were close to taking Kesh.

To the south of the valley, past Kesh there were three lakes connected by narrow strips of land that met at the village of Katra. In the event that the defenses in Kesh caved in these lakes would make the enemy passage slightly more difficult and a contingent of well-armed men may well delay the advance or progress of the invaders. The defense of the area around the lakes and the village of Katra was tasked to Captain Shahnameh and a fifteen thousand strong army of volunteers and mercenaries who were moved from their garrison in Anantnag.

Azag's difficulties were further compounded by the onset of winter which arrived earlier than normal that year. Chunks of ice delayed his progress and the soldiers lacked the necessary gear required to sustain a protracted war effort in winter conditions. The cold weather coupled with continuous rain turned the mud tracks that zigzagged across the landscape into unusable traps. The harsh Lamunian winter where conditions could fall well below freezing point further hampered refurbishments of the frontlines. The rafts that were crossing the Zohreb were occasionally scuttled by frozen lumps of ice.

Inevitably preparations for the siege of Kesh were delayed until there was some respite from the winter conditions. While Azag was stalled by sleet, snow, rain and mild blizzards powered by strong winds, Natasha seized the opportunity and worked frantically to improve her defenses.

Natasha seized the opportunity and worked frantically to improve her defenses.

By mid-winter most of the defensive positions had been extensively fortified. There were in addition to the line that stretched from Kesh to the fringes of the eastern Reasi forest four other horizontal lines that helped bolster the defenses of Lamunia. Natasha emphasized less on the forested areas on either side of the Zohreb and concentrated principally on the more open and accessible plains in the south. Many of the men in Dadgem and Pulwara, the volunteers in Anantnag and the Engineering Corps in Shupiyan spent the early winter days taking closer order of their defenses.

In the meantime Captain Niaz's rancorous army kept pushing forward bolstered by endless reinforcements that crossed the river at all hours but the spearhead of his attack was repeatedly blunted by counter offensives and the death toll kept mounting.

It was inevitable that a collapse would precipitate a counter attack by Shahnameh. On the verge of buckling, Captain Niaz's men eventually reached Katra but were repelled by fresh troops from the Fourth and Fifth Corps. The volunteers fought well alongside the mercenaries and the enemy had no choice but to pull back and by so doing Niaz forfeited any gains that they had made. The fighting was so intense that the ground was soaked in blood.

Following the withdrawal the battle shifted to the eastern sector of the valley. The retreating soldiers cut across the dense forest and came in direct contact for the first time with the line that refurbished Azardokth's men and in so doing managed to inadvertently cut off the supply line from the south causing the assault on the enemy crossing to come to a halt and allowing Azag to land additional troops on the shores of the Zohreb. The reinforcements swung immediately into action.

As wave upon wave of enemy troops came ashore the momentum began to swing Azag's way and the defenders were soon pushed south and retreated towards the Lamunian-Amestrian border. The line from Kesh that stretched to the northernmost slopes of the eastern forest could no longer be sustained. Many of the men scurried to a retreat after being cut off and many lost their lives.

Azag more by providence than skill coordinated the landings well and the unplanned assault on Azardokth halted the rain of rocks and other shrapnel that had so tormented them. His second in command Azi Dahaka showing some skill did not press the advantage but concentrated on securing the perimeters and beachheads allowing the defenders to take the initiative. Within three days Azag launched another offensive, first towards Kesh and then onwards to Pulwara and Masada Fort.

Azardokth in the meantime, confronted by overwhelming odds and unable to contain the threat any longer set the catapults alight reducing the siege engines that had served her so well to ashes and retreated southeast in an attempt to regroup with Natasha's southern front.

Four days later Kesh was captured but a large number of mercenaries and volunteers had escaped to the east. Azag was caught up in a deadly game of cat and mouse. He prepared to follow up his victory in Kesh with another offensive on Katra and Pulwara but was hampered by bad weather and he was forced to adopt a defensive posture while he waited for the weather to improve.

Natasha V

The reinforcements in Reasi and the additional landings were part of Azag's strategic offensive which took place on all permissible fronts. The Lamunian defenses fought back with tenacity throwing everything they could muster at the enemy. Hawk's Nest in response mobilized additional troops to help bolster the defenses in the southern flatlands.

The battle shifted from Kesh to the eastern sector of Lamunia, to Pulwara and Masada fort. From Kesh, Azag's men cut southeast thereby avoiding a confrontation with the Emerald Knights stationed at Dadgem opting instead to target Masada Fort. Azag wanted to take the fort intact and use it as his new base of operations in Lamunia.

Natasha mobilized her remaining horse lancers in Western Dadgem to cut off Azag's offensive. Azag was a strategist whose strengths lay in battle formations and tactical maneuvers. The ragged guerilla style warfare that the defenders opted for and the sometimes rugged, inhospitable terrain did not suit him. Despite his shortcomings he admittedly fared better than most.

As wave upon wave of Azag's men came ashore those at the front were inevitable pushed further inland and a long line stretched from the banks of the Zohreb to Kesh, Katra and Pulwara in the southeast. The Emerald Knights who rode in support of the horse lancers tried to cut off the lines and attempted to form a wedge between the columns. The princess herself rode in the lead.

Unlike her men Natasha forgo any armor and dressed instead in loose fitting silk garments. She had a sword strapped to her side and a bow slung across her shoulders with a quiver of arrows latched to her back. She wore a golden reef around her head and because of the armor she had been gifted at birth she was impervious to mortal attacks.

Azag's men scurried to a retreat as they were unexpectedly cut off between Kesh and Katra and in so doing lost most of their armored vehicles which were set alight with torches after being doused with kerosene and vegetable oil. The men inside were either burnt to death by the flames or cut down by horse lancers and archers when they tried to break out of the wooden coffins.

Natasha coordinated her attacks well causing Azag to hemorrhage both men and equipment. By the start of the following month Hawk's Nest had bolstered its numbers in Lamunia. Azardokht was back with Golnaz as her deputy together with a new contingent of archers at her disposal. With the support of mobile units they started to harrow and harass Azag's flanks. His men without their armored vehicles began to lose their bite and fell prey to trained archers and lancers. A counter attack was clearly on the cards and the storm gathered force. Azag could do little but wait. The anticipated attack started within a fortnight. It was a concerted assault on all fronts more successful in the east against an ill prepared Niaz.

Azag however was a wily veteran and was able to outmaneuver the attack effectively. He reinforced the lines with additional divisions and deployed archers of his own, who unlike the defenders used crossbows that were particularly damaging to men on horses. The intense fighting continued through winter when the Lamunian offensive came to a halt, due to soft ground caused by spring graining in and melting snow.

The muddy ground made infantry mobility difficult and the counter attack came to a temporary standstill. The horse lancers who were more heavily armored than the rest were bogged down. The additional armor that they carried despite giving them an aura of formidability restricted mobility. A week later the ground began to freeze again allowing Natasha to refurbish her lines and renew the offensive. The attack began anew on the thirteenth day of the third month of the new year along all fronts with robust efforts in the east where the Lamunians had been most successful.

Azag realized that if he was to salvage any hope of remaining in Lamunia he needed to double his reinforcements. He sent in divisions of highly skilled horsemen to counter the horse lancers and mobile divisions to strengthen the conquest of Lamunia.

By the third week of the month the defenders were battered into withdrawal. New offensives were launched the following week but the attack could not make much ground and was rebuked in a matter of days. By the mid of the fourth month both sides were deadlocked in a grating battle. Natasha's troops held their positions while Azag's men took the initiative only to be repelled.

Azag paused to plan his summer campaign and he decided to center his efforts once again on Masada Fort. Its capture he decided was crucial to the long term success of his mission. In addition to its strategic location, the fort also held storage facilities that were vital to the continued campaign in Lamunia, which at present looked to last at least another winter. He sought every possible advantage to compensate for his weaknesses. He enlisted the help of engineers and like Azardokth had done earlier, he started building catapults. A specialized ground support force was positioned to support the siege engines.

Azag's persistence in Lamunia underlined the strategic importance of the kingdom and its capture was paramount for the Dark Lord to stand any chance of defeating Hawk's Nest. Azag's immediate task was to take Pulwara and if the flow of battle stayed its course, Azag would launch an offensive and Natasha would absorb the attack and eventually negate any gains that Azag had made. The princess seemed content to hold out.

Azag's summer campaign was launched on the eight day of the fifth month and went according to plan. Azag's men retaliated on all fronts and almost every Lamunian division was caught up in the action. Natasha stuck to her strategy. Her men held their ground and organized incisive counter attacks but then the fates conspired against them and Azag summoned the help of evil pairikās or fairies to his aid. Like the elves, the fairies were divided into benevolent and compassionate fairies who bestowed wealth and good fortune and evil fairies who were harbingers of sickness, plagues and epidemics. Many of her men fell victim to a plague that spread through the encampments like wildfire.

Three days later Azag's men reach Masada Fort. They pushed on and men on both sides fought to the last drop. Niaz's plan to infuse the body of his men with the spirits of the dead finally paid off and his troops impervious to pain fought like madmen. The defenders that rallied around

Masada Fort were crushed. Farazmon was captured and beheaded after being subjected to brutal torture. Masoud was left to defend the fort on his own. Standing to confront him were large tapered towers on wheels filled with archers that the enemy had managed to maneuver into position.

Natasha was left without choice. She had to mobilize the backbone of her army, the twenty three thousand five hundred imperial guards under the command of Captain Zavareh. The reinforcements that Hawk's Nest had sent her were unable to stem the tide.

With Masada under siege Azag turned his attentions to Dadgem. His ploy was simply to batter the city with everything he had and reduce the resistance to rubble. He began ferrying more men and equipment across the Zohreb and imploring the Dark Lord to provide him with every possible resource.

The defenders in the meantime had not been ideal and had increased their fortifications around Dadgem. The defenses included ditches, traps and wire entanglements to offset Azag's onslaught. Hundreds of traps had been set up thanks to supplies that were constantly ferried in from the Betan Plateau.

Azag was in two minds. He could not risk pulling back his forces back from Masada to supplement his men who were trying to wrest control of Dadgem from the defenders. There was no news of Khasham who was trapped in the western forest that was nothing less than a strategic backwater to say the least. Azag was uncertain if the captain and his men were still alive or had been driven to madness and rued the decision to send him into the forest.

Azag was ordered to secure Dadgem in return for more reinforcements and supplies. Faced with no other option, he committed thirty thousand fighting fit men to the task comprising of men from his regular units. The defenders were welled up in a small area and the best tactic to deploy was to shrink the enemy's size by intense and repeated attacks.

The defenders at Dadgem were determined and given their proficiency and superiority in battle an infantry attack favored the horsemen. Bearing this in mind the Emerald Knights began to goad Azag's men into launching heedless frontal attacks by posting inciting and provocative signs; bait to see if the enemy would bite. Azag snapped at it and sent his men into a headlong attack and the invaders streamed through from all directions.

He supported the attack with repeated aerial bombardments by bringing his catapults into action which began on the second day of the sixth month. The initial targets were permanent fortifications that could easily be crushed with stones. The defenders were subjected to a spate of repeated barrages and many of their fortifications crumbled during the early stages of battle. The infantry attack began the next day but as expected it was a grim struggle, with the tide of battle flowing back and forth reminiscent of the battles that had been fought in the previous months.

After ten days of bitter and extensive fighting, Azag's battalions at Dadgem were exhausted and some numbered a mere few hundred men. They had little choice but to replace some of their units with those from Masada and in the process weakened the attack on the fort. The additional troops helped and by the middle of the sixth month they had made headway.

Azag's aerial artillery now dominated the fortifications at Dadgem but that did not stop the supplies from streaming in. Members of the buoyant outfit from the Betan Plateau had managed to secure a route from the south and carted in supplies from the rear which included arms, food and medication.

It was at this stage that Azag proved his genius. He ordered his men to launch an all out attack from entrenched positions, throwing caution to the wind. The blistering attack knocked the Lamunians off balance and the defenders were caught off guard. It was a daring attack and cutting across well defended areas was difficult to say the least but Azag was adamant and attempted the unexpected. The element of surprise was always crucial to success.

He had managed to get his troops in position under the cover of darkness and the weary knights failed to spot the danger. The defenders lost ground at an alarming rate and were soon pushed back to old war fortifications that remained from the days of the Empire. Dadgem was captured within days.

The evacuation of Dadgem began on the last day of the month. Those that were fortunate enough to have horses and those that were able to walk soon started moving south. Some chose to remain behind to give the escapees enough time to get a head start and they continued to fight to their deaths.

———◆———

Dadgem was taken and Masada was under siege. According to all reports it would not be able to hold out until winter.

The retreating troops poisoned wells and destroyed crop fields. Not a single morsel of food was to be made available to the enemy. What remained of the horse lancers, Emerald Knights, archers and foot-soldiers regrouped under the Imperial Guards led by Captain Zavareh on the southern front. Iradeh, Azardokht and Golnaz survived the battles. Captain Masoud was trapped in Masada and there was no foreseeable escape for him. Natasha was still in command of the defenses and she contemplated a counter attack but word had arrived from Hawk's Nest to the contrary.

The southern front was to hold out for the rest of the year and a new frontline was formed just before the Lamunian-Amestrain border. Lamunia was a foregone conclusion and it was only foreseeable that the enemy will push their way south towards Amestria once Masada was taken.

◆━◈━◆

Azag's siege of Masada Fort began in late autumn. After having overpowered the out-forts located at the bottom of the spur, Azag took a closer look at the castle's location, its towers and triple set of walls. A frontal assault would have been very costly, so he resorted to a solution commonly used during castle sieges: a complete blockade, precipitating famine within the stronghold that would eventually force the garrison to surrender.

He completely isolated the fortress using two lines of defenses: the circumvallation* and the contravallation**. These two lines comprised of ditches fitted with stockades

---

*   *A network of fortifications set up by and surrounding the besiegers in order to confront possible reinforcements*

**   *A network of entrenchments around a stronghold in order to prevent any sorties by the besieged or the defenders*

protected by wooden spiked posts planted to the ground and towered platforms for archers. The first line, the circumvallation, looked like an enclosure on the opposite side of the fortress. It was designed to defend against potential sorties.

The second line, the contravallation, was designed to prevent any reinforcements from running through the blockade that had been imposed.

Masada Fort was surrounded by a moat and only a narrow path linked the castle to the rest of the surrounding terrain where Azag stationed his army. Once the fortress was completely surrounded Azag's troops settled down for the winter and busied themselves with building siege engines.

The siege continued for seven months and in that time Azag's men waited patiently and watched relentlessly, mocking the beleaguered captain and his men daily. As the siege continued to drag on there was a growing despair that the siege soldiers would grow weary and start deserting.

Azag's army had been weakened by the continuous fighting in the west and columns had to ferry back and forth. He also had to consider the possibility that reinforcements might arrive and counter his plans forcing his army to abandon the siege and that weighed heavily on his mind.

Taking into account all the above factors Azag decided it was time to storm the castle. The only viable location from which to launch an offensive was a plateau overlooking the castle, which was linked to the fortress by a narrow dirt path.

The attack was launched from this vantage point towards one of the fortified gate-houses. The first step was to build wooden causeways that would enable the aggressors to approach without being hit by missiles that had been cast or hurled by the defenders.

The moat was then progressively filled with divots, stones, fascines and earth carried in baskets. The soldiers sought protection under wooden structures mounted on wheels and covered with fire proof materials. This allowed them to advance without sustaining injuries from the defenders missiles. They also sought shelter behind mantelets and retaliated with bricoles. In the meantime the tapered tower was brought forward.

From the wooden tower archers sent showers of arrows and hurled stones and debris at the defenders. Masoud's men retaliated with hails of missiles slung from their slingshots and volleys of arrows of their own directed at the attackers and the soldiers inside the gallery. Heavy boulders and wooden beams were also used.

Some of Azag's deranged men couldn't wait for the moat to be filled. They clambered across it and set up ladders along the counterscarp. The ladder however was too short and they used their hands and swords to scramble upwards. None of them reached the top.

Once the moat was filled out, the sappers, heavily protected, reached the foot of the castle tower and started digging or mining, working on the flanks and the foundations of the tower, under the cover of shields that protected them from the hail of arrows that was fired from overhead.

Thus covered, they hid in the depth of the walls, after having excavated beneath. They then filled out the holes with tree trunks fearing that the higher portion of the wall could come crashing down on them. Once the opening was large enough they set fire to the trunks and withdrew to a safer location.

The tower collapsed with a great noise, sending up a huge cloud of dust and created an opening inside the wall. Sensing that it was useless to stay inside the fortified gate-house any longer, the defenders set fire to the building to slow down the progress of the enemy and retreated to the next enclosure.

Azag's soldiers managed to stamp out the fire and they occupied the deserted gate-house without delay. They then had to negotiate another deeper larger ditch that surrounded the first enclosure. The men were about to commence with a second siege when a slice of good fortune came their way.

The previous king, Vaspar the Beneficent, had quite carelessly built a temple along the inner part of the southern wall which had an opening towards the outside. The openings were low enough for the enemy to scale with a small ladder and the distinguished Captain had completely forgotten to block up or watch the particular opening.

The fatal mistake would lead to his downfall. Azag's men entered the building, through the opening, and hauled their companions inside with a rope. Soon at least twenty men had made their way into the interior of the temple and they tried to smash the doors to gain access to the courtyard.

Hearing the commotion the defenders piled heaps of wood at the entrance just before the door and set the bundle alight to try and chase the enemy away or at least to prevent them from entering the lower courtyard. But the fire spread to the neighboring buildings and the smoke grew so thick and intense that it troubled the defenders.

They abandoned the enclosure that could no longer be defended, and retreated to the following enclosure. Azag's men smashed down the door and braving the fire they ran towards the entrance and severed the ropes of the drawbridge which fell and opened the way for the rest for the men who were waiting on the other side and the first enclosure was taken.

Masoud and his men sought refuge in the next enclosure but he lost at least one third of his men in doing so. The attackers erected wooden shields in front of the enclosure's gate and started, under cover, to excavate a new mine to hasten the collapse of the wall.

The defenders started digging a counter-mine of their own that would lead to the sapper's gallery. Azag in response loosed the buckets on the catapults that flung large boulders at the wall. The continuous pounding finally caused part of the wall to collapse. (The wall had already been weakened beneath by the mining and counter-mining galleries).

Masoud bravely retaliated with his men to prevent an attack through the breach and a violent hand to hand battle ensued. The attackers overwhelmed the defenders by sheer numbers and the men defending the castle slowly perished.

Masoud and the remainder of his men tried to make a getaway but they were surrounded from all directions. Outnumbered and cut off from their last possible retreat and too exhausted to fight any further they surrendered. After a seven month siege Azag had managed to capture Masada Fort. Masoud and the remainder of his men were executed.

Natasha VI

--- ❖ ---

Natasha climbed the white steps that were located just past a cascading natural fountain that was bubbling with effervescent water from an underground stream. The princess had taken a leave of absence and despite the bitter battle that raged in the south of Lamunia, she felt the overwhelming urge to pay a visit to the temple that stood within the confines of the sacred forest. The forest was hidden from all mortals shrouded by a veil of magic and it was only visible to the highest ranking members of the Order of Dawn. It was located in the Highlands of Geancanach.

The steps led the way towards an open door and she walked past a set of marble pillars that stood like guard towers on either side of the doorway before she entered. The pillars separated the roof from the base of the temple and a set of four pillars were neatly aligned in prim rows on all four sides of the temple. The entire structure was painted a frosty white and looked untouched and unscarred by human hands. The door to the temple remained opened at all times and as one entered the temple they were greeted by a large fire shrine that stood boldly in the middle facing the doorway erected on a floor inlaid with gold.

The shrine remained alight throughout the day and the smoke that drifted upwards from the fire escaped through a circular vent that was ideally position at the pinnacle of the white domed temple and escaped into the wide open sky. The walls of the temple were inlaid with precious stones that were arranged in a manner that depicted rare flowers on a background of glistening gold and approximately eight cubits behind the shrine there was a larger than life statute of Dawn. The distance between the doorway and the statute was approximately twenty cubits.

The gem-stoned interior of the temple was brought to life by the dazzling light of the sun that streamed through the flat glass spheres that were strategically positioned around the dome to bring to light the magical colors of each gemstone. The princess walked through the door and knelt before a dais that was located just in front of the fire shrines. She held her head low revering the flames of Mainyu Athra. A tiny wind drifted in through the open door and the flame of the fire shrine dance to the breeze in reply to Natasha's prayers. It was a sign to let the princess know that Athra had heard her.

Natasha stood up and walked past the shrine keeping her head low, as she did so, not wanting to sully the flames of Athra in anyway. As she walked past the shrine the wind disappeared and the flame was upright once again.

She continued walking, head still held low, until she reached the altar of Dawn. A cubit or so in front of the altar, on a slightly elevated platform that stretched for the breadth of the altar, were trays of ambrosia, comprising of rare forest sweets and fruits, blessed by the elder who resided in the interior of the temple. Anyone who was fortunate enough to find their way to the temple was welcome to partake in the feast that was laid out on the platform in front of the altar and drink their fill from the fountain outside. If by chance they did eat the fruits from the altar of Dawn and drink the water from the fountain of youth, they'd cease aging, if not for an eternity then at least temporarily.

Natasha went down on her knees again, head down and lifted a nectarine from the golden tray before she bit into it. As she munched away she felt all traces of tiredness and tenebrosity disappear. The troubles that had clouded her spirit in recent times miraculously vanished. She lifted her head and looked at the life like image of Dawn, one of the four prettiest goddesses in the known world. She couldn't help but sigh in contentment at her breathtaking beauty. A golden leaf fell from the circlet around the goddess's head gently swaying to an unseen breeze on its way down and landed before her knees. The fallen leaf was a sign that Dawn responded kindly to the unspoken compliment. Natasha instantly felt vivified.

She was a blessed child, favored by the Goddess in many ways and when she gazed at the statute she felt herself at peace. The features of Dawn shimmered away by the light of the sacred fire and together Dawn and Athra were the twin lights that washed away all fear and doubt, the darkness that often clouded corporeal perceptions.

Dressed in an armor of dazzling gold Dawn blazed away in the company of Athra and the pair with their resuscitating light touched and revived anyone who had been struck by the rigors of life. Natasha bowed her head once again and repeated a prayer to the goddess before she stood up and walked to the rear of the temple.

Just to the extreme right of the wall behind the statute of Dawn there stood a wooden oak door that looked like it had been given a fresh coat of paint and as she approached the fragrance of sweet, scented wood permeated the air. She tapped lightly on the door; she knew that there was someone behind it, seated at a mahogany table inspecting scrolls written on papyrus and parchment.

"Enter" said a soft musical voice and she turned the golden door knob before she pushed the door backwards. As she did so, she saw a man whose skin was as pale as the goddess she worshipped. He was tall and slim almost four and a half cubits in height with a long white beard that reached down to his chest. He was dressed in long silken white robes. Natasha had met the man before. His name was Nereiðr and if by chance one got close enough to him they'd realize that he had pointy years. He looked up from his reading and greeted her with a warm smile. Natasha ran over to him and gave the elf a hug just as he pushed his chair back to stand up and greet her.

Nereiðr was a light elf and the sacred woods were some of the few remaining light elf sanctuaries. The elves lived in the woods and built their dwellings on trees and branches. In the beginning they were as many elves as they were men but their numbers were depleted following the battle before time.

He looked at her with his pale blue eyes that reflected the wisdom of the ages and paused before she spoke. "What ails you my daughter?" he asked. Natasha remained silent. Nereiðr knew the answer to the question well before asking it but he went through the motions hoping that he could make her talk but the princess remained tight lipped and an unobtrusive silence ensued.

Nereiðr shrugged his shoulders and threw his hands up in the air. "Well if you're going to give up that easily maybe he was wrong in appointing you in the first place" he said. Natasha gave him a steely glare. "You know well enough that I only took it upon myself to lead his army because I was filled with a sense of duty. I felt that it was my responsibility to defend the citizens of Lamunia" she said. "Fiddlesticks" said Nereiðr. Natasha looked aggrieved or at least she tried to.

"You took charge because you wanted to show him that you were a capable and competent leader" he said. "You could have refused but you didn't, did you?" he asked. Natasha hesitated before she blurted out rather bluntly "well it doesn't matter now does it?" she snapped back before breaking into a giggle. "How well you see through me Nereiðr" she said. "I'm like your father, I know everything about you little one" he said.

"I guess you know all about the battle then?" she asked her mood suddenly thoughtful. Nereiðr nodded his head "There wasn't much you could do, you were outnumbered". "Is there any way I can defeat Azag?" she asked the underlying tones of uncertainty clearly evident in her voice. Nereiðr smiled. "I was just thinking of that my child" he said. "There may be a way".

He returned to his chair and assumed the look of a man bursting with answers. "Have you heard of dragon lore?" he asked. Natasha shook her head. "No matter I will explain" said Nereiðr. "The dragon mages of the elven race keep it a secret so I don't blame you for not knowing it. Even with the elven race it is known only to a select few". "Dragon lore unravels the mysteries of the dragon race, the sons of Dragos, who are not of this world. They are five different types of dragons, the progenitors of their kind. There is the red fire breather, the green earth dweller, the blue water dragon, the white frost dragon and the pale wind drifter. The dragon mages share the mind of these flighted dragons from the time they are hatched and in this manner they share the thoughts of the dragons. For each dragon hatched there is a group of five dragon mages who are assigned to share the collective consciousness of the dragon. Inevitably they become inexplicably linked to the dragons".

"Little is known of dragon world. It is located in a constellation which lies in the farthest reaches of space but it is known that Dragos is the lord protector of the dragon race". "None of the dragon mages have been able to share the mind of Dragos and all those who have tried have come to a bitter end".

"The scribes of the dragon mages also narrate the tale of the serpent-eels who are distinct from the children of Dragos, and I will tell it to you. Store it well in your memory child". "The serpent-eels are children of the godless ones in whose veins run the blood of that which slithers at the feet of the negative aspect of the Brahmatma". "The accursed ones vary in sizes and the smaller ones, the more cunning of their race are cradle snatchers. They have seized thousands of infants from their cots of birth and have bred them to become emissaries of darkness".

"The serpent-eels are nothing like the dragons. They are eel like beasts of varying lengths with smooth slippery skin as opposed to the skin of the true-bloods, the sons of Dragos, which is hard and scaly".

"The serpent-eels inhabit the smoldering pits of the underworld; they exist in underground caverns and in the muddied marshes of the dark forests in Irkalla. Unlike the true bloods that constantly seek to bask in the light of the sun, for Dragos himself is as radiant as the sun in all aspects, the serpent-eels prefer to slither in the darkness of the night."

"Deep within the caverns of Mount Kieddoaivi groups of dragon mages live in underground grottos and share the thoughts of the dragons that were born in the known world. There were in total five dragons that were hatched within the confines of the Kieddoaivi. Of the five only the wind-drifter remains in this world; the others have wandered off to distant galaxies. The dragon however hasn't been sighted in centuries and according to the dragon mages it slumbers away in the snow clad peaks of a distant mountain, deep in transcendental sleep. The wind-drifter is the most spiritual of its kind".

"Aesthetically pious the creature has entered a comatose state and has ceased all physical activity choosing instead to probe the universe with its mind. Sharing the consciousness of the dragon meant that the mages themselves entered a similar condition and regressed into a state of deep meditation. It is through this natural process of spiritual acquisition that the mages were initially able to garner information about the dragon world".

"Like you child, all dragons are solar entities. If you were able to gain access to the consciousness of the wind-drifter then with its help, you'll be able defeat Azag". Natasha remained silent and listened keenly to what Nereiðr had to say her interests peeked.

"Well?" asked Nereiðr. "Well what??" responded Natasha uncertain of what Nereiðr had in mind. The elf sighed and continued "Would you like to meet the dragon mages who shared the consciousness of the wind drifter?". A smile instantly lit the princess's face and she nodded her head with excitement.

Ναταsha VII

During the journey to Mount Kieddoaivi, Natasha managed to get a good look around the sacred forest. It stretched for as far as the eye could see and instead of tall trees and clumps of bushes that were peculiar to forests in the region, it comprised of vast meadows that stretched eastwards, inundated with homes and villages peculiar to elves and pastures littered with grazing animals. Dikes had been raised by incessant labor on the shores of meandering rivers to shut out the turbulent tides and the flood gates were only opened to accommodate the changing of seasons.

To the west and south there were fields of wheat, corn, and flax spreading afar and to the east there were orchards, open and unfenced stretching over the plains. To the north stood bold mountains that overlooked happy valleys and lush green trees dotted the hills on either side of the valley with leaves boasting a diverse range of colors.

On the hills and the plains there were houses that were firmly built, with frames of oak and cedar, thatched with straw roofs and gilded chimneys that stood upright with dormer-windows and projecting gables that protected and shaded the doorways. There in the tranquil evenings of summer when sunset brightly lit the sky, elves would gather around and exchange tales of old.

Matrons and maidens dressed in snow-white caps and kirtles, the color of blue, yellow and green busied themselves with distaffs spinning the golden flax for the gossiping looms amidst the squeaks of noisy shutters and shutting doors caused by fleeting winds mingled with the whir of the wheels and the songs of the maidens.

Somewhat distant from the houses, close to a basin, a shepherd dwelt on the goodly acres of a farmer keeping a keen eye on the flock of sheep that he tended. Never taking his eyes off the flock for a moment, he watched as his sheep fed from the early hours of the morning until midday when he guided his sheep to the shade and allowed himself a quick snooze beneath the shade of tall trees.

The princess got a good look around and she saw the house of a farmer firmly built with rafters of oak. It stood on a commanding hill in the shade of a steady sycamore wreathed with woodbine.

The house had a porch that was coarsely decorated with seats and stood at the end of a well travelled footpath that lead through an orchard to a lush green meadow filled with grass and dainty flowers. Farther down the path was a well with a moss-grown bucket fastened to a rope attached to a wooden arm and near it a trough for the horses. Shielding the house from storms, on the north, was a barn and just in front of it was a farm-yard and on it stood the broad-wheeled wains, the antique ploughs and the harrows.

The lordly turkey strutted and the cock crowed while the hen ran helter-skelter pecking away at its dinner as the ducks trudged in an orderly line to the pool. The barn was bursting with hay and the gable projected a thatched roof and a staircase under the sheltering eaves that led up to the odorous corn-loft. Dove-cots were clearly visible on some of the roofs with meek inmates murmuring incessantly. On the ridges, in a gusty breeze noisy weathercocks spun and rattled to a snazzy tune.

The road that led to the mountains turned away from the scenic paradise and steeped up a slope along lanes bordered by beds of shrubberies, filled with flowers of all kinds in between pines, cedars, birches and sycamores. The fragrance that the flowers exuded declared the forest vibrant and alive. Inhaling its ardent aroma the princess was suffused with the exuberance of a child. The fragrant scent that wafted from the wondrous blossoms made her feel truly like a queen. The toil of war and the fatigue of battle disappeared without a lingering trace and as she walked beside Nereiðr she felt the calmness that had eluded her in recent times evaporate and in its stead stood the peace and serenity of contentment. Divinity she decided must reside in this forest.

Overlooking the grasslands, the mountains of the elven forest stood tall and firm, protecting all life, both big and small. Right in the middle flanked by smaller mountains on either side stood Mount Kieddoaivi. The glimmering icicles that decorated its peaks could be seen from afar shimmering like crystals in the blazing light of the sun.

They continued their journey without stop nor rest, for neither were discomforted by the pangs of tiredness, thirst or hunger, and soon they felt the soft dew that preceded the setting sun touch their skin. A calm breeze drifted their way and the blades of grass that grew like carpets on the gentle grime and graveled floor at the slopes of the mountains swayed to the soft wind as the fading light bounced off the soft, green beads of dew that sat gently on the stalks.

She looked above at the sky that stared blankly back at her to admire the soft pillowy clouds that wandered freely as it replaced the blue of the day with the orange of twilight and she spotted the first twinkles of the early stars that came out to bid the solar barge a fond adieu as it sailed into the harbor.

The path to the mountains led up a winding slope and as they progressed further into their journey the trees grew wider and farther apart. The lush green of grass was replaced by the languishing brown of dirt and gravel. It times of old Kieddoaiv served as a mountain fortress, the final unassailable bastion that stood firm after a prolonged battle. When all was almost lost the elves withdrew to the scraggy retreat.

"The belly of Kieddoaiv is filled with molten lava and it is from its liquid metal thats the dwarf workmen forged the swords and shields of elven warriors" said Nereiðr. Natasha thought ruefully back at her own weapons that were forged by the blacksmiths of Mirkash and realized that she was at a complete disadvantage. It was however not possible for mortals to acquire elven weapons for only the elves could bear them.

As they drew closer the Kieddoaiv loomed ahead like a tall bold castle, its summit dark and misty. Even if one was to look at it in the brazen light of noon a cloud of white magical mist phlegmatically crowned the peaks that towered above all else.

The slopes close to the summit were adorned with pure timeless crystals of ice and flakes of pristine snow. Steep and vertiginous in the whistling wind, it stood a lonesome crest with trees closer to the summit shivering in the vivid cold, striped of their leaves, permitting the world to revel in their naked bodies. The onset of night did nothing to diminish the silence that lingered in the air. It was not a desolate silence nor was it a forlorn silence but it was the silence of peace and contentment, the silence of rest and reprieve.

As the day grew darker and night approached the stars started filtering through dazzling in their brilliance. The moon weary from its climb to the summit sprawled to rest in the company of wandering stars lighting the way forward.

The walk was soothing and the pair talked as they plodded along. Natasha's mind drifted away from strategic thinking and the other concerns that had subjugated her like a burden that could not be lifted from her shoulders. She talked and walked freely un-lumbered and unencumbered. The path grew steeper but because she had eaten the fruit from the altar of Dawn she felt neither the strain nor the exertion that normally accompanied an uphill climb.

The veil of the night soon lifted and Dawn ushered in the light of morn. The young princess looked up to stare at the lofty crown of the Kieddoaiv in the light of the tangerine sky that had come to bless away the trepidations of the night. Natasha stood still to bathe in the early light and brought her plams together holding them upright just below her chin and uttered a prayer to greet the goddess of infinite grace, wisdom and beauty. They continued to walk up the steep, ragged slope, across gurgling mountain streams that cut across the rocks, greeted by a flutter of white doves that went in search of their morning meal.

The rocks of the Kieddoaivi stood in aged splendor with lives that spanned eons. These rocks were undoubtedly alive. Natasha could feel the farvashi, the spiritual component that existed it all objects, animate and inanimate, emanate from the stones. She felt certain that the rocks whispered in silence and talked discreetly to each other. If she could only hear them speak, they would have told her the secrets of the ages and help her unravel the sacred threads that held the cosmos together. Wedged between the crevices, embraced in arms of rocks, there were fissures that oozed tears distressed perhaps at the fate that awaited mortal kind.

With the death of every elf or the demise of every celestial and heavenly being the known world lost a pinch of white magic for these creatures were not only magical entities but beings that kept the quantities of white magic in the known world intact. It could be that the battle before time was orchestrated to balance the quantities of the white magic with the quantities of black magic in the atmosphere or perhaps in was the intention of the Brahmatma that all things should be equal.

She knelt to the ground again and pressed her check against the rough lichen that grew indiscriminately. It felt like the thorny beard of her father and discreet sounds became audible to her ears. She tried in vain to discern the whispers of rocks from the growls that filled the bowels of the earth but soon gave up trying.

Beneath the earth molten lava rolled and roiled, turning and toiling. The bubbly crackles released clouds of vapor that escaped through tiny crevasses and permeated through to the surface. Lifting her head from the ground the princess said to Nereiðr "she sounds angry". "Nay child" he said "she merely huffs and puffs". "Kieddoaivi is a placid mountain and she wouldn't hurt anyone" said the elf elder. They continued their climb up the steep incline until they reached an opening which resembled the mouth of a cave. Nereiðr led the way and the princess followed close behind. They entered a passage that was lit by torches nimbly balanced on steep ledges. Outside, day had broken and sunlight streamed through in full force.

The passage was narrow but could easily fit four men walking beside each other. The air was alight with the color of red tangerine. The granite walls on either side were chiseled smooth and with the exception of the faint glistening of ores, they were plain without any lingering traces of markings.

The path continued downwards and an hour or so into their journey they began to hear the faint echoes of chipping shovels. "The dwarfs are working" explained Nereiðr. As they progressed further inwards the sounds grew louder.

"What are they doing?" asked Natasha unable to contain her curiosity any longer. "They are mining, looking for precious ore that is used in the forging and molding of weapons" said Nereiðr. "The caverns of the dragon mages are located in the grottos below. The mages haven't seen the light of day in centuries. Their minds are deeply connected to that of the wind-drifter" the elf continued. The mages have been in transcendental sleep for as long as the dragon that they are mentally adjoined to" replied Nereiðr. "We'd have to wake the mages and the wind-drifter up. The dragon would be famished because it hasn't eaten for centuries". "As soon as it arises, it would want to eat" he added in a cautious tone that sounded like a gentle warning.

"Dragons had voracious appetites and when they fed they consumed only meat and that too in huge quantities. But when they entered a meditative state their hunger abated. It is by sharing the collective thoughts of the dragons that the elven mages learned of dragon magic which is transcribed in an archaic form of writing stored in the inner labyrinths of their mind" he continued.

Natasha pondered over what she had just heard and she responded with the first question that came to her mind.

"How would we feed him once we awaken him?" she asked. "We won't have to he will feed himself" replied Nereiðr.

"I remember it, the wind-drifter, from long ago" he continued. "Its wings stretched from one tip to the other for approximately one hundred and thirty nine cubits and its body was at least one hundred and forty nine cubits in length. When it spread its wings in flight small farms would be engulfed in total darkness. It was an impressive sight. Its body was the pale of aether and its scales glistened in the blaze of the shimmering sun. It loved the heat. Like all the sons of Dragos, it liked nothing better than to laze in the glory of the effulgent sun".

"Its scales are as cold as shining ice but glisten continuously like an ever flickering flame. In its chest it held the flames many times that of a burning hearth. Its eyeballs were the color of its scales and its claws resembled talons many times the size of a hawk. It was able to lacerate even the sturdiest rock with a mere scratch. Its face held a radiance so bright that it could blind a lesser mortal". "With its nostrils it could smell dread and with its tongue it could taste fear. Its mind held wisdom like no other".

"It resided on the summit of a lofty mountain, close to the sky, in a temple crafted from the blood red gold of demons and inlaid with jewels and other treasures that it looted and plundered from the demon kings during the battle before time".

ΠΑΤΑSHA VIII

◈

They continued to walk down the swerving passage that was covered with soft delicate sand, guided by the unwavering light of torches. Minutes later Natasha caught her first glimpse of a dwarf. They were approximately half the size of full grown elves but bulkier and on their shoulders they held picks or shovels. Many had beards that reached down to their tummies and a thick leather belt wrapped around their waist adorned with large silver buckles. The bowed their heads and murmured a greeting that was barely audible when they caught sight of Nereiðr.

Some who were much bolder than others pursed their lips together and let out little whistles as soon as they saw Natasha. "My, my" said a voice from within the tunnel, "what a pretty lass" said another, "I'm in love" said yet another and the young princess continued to receive compliments as she made her way down the tunnel. Natasha couldn't help but blush. Well if these dwarfs ever needed a home they certainly had one in Mirkash. "What wonderful people" said Natasha to the elf elder and Nereiðr nodded his head.

The princess put on her prettiest smile, "the colors of her cheeks will make roses turn pale with envy" said a distant voice, "and from her heart rich with compassion, she sends out a wailing fragrance" echoed another. "If perchance her perfumed tress be allowed to flitter to the wind's caress, the hyacinths would complain and languish in sweet distress" continued another. Natasha's face started to glow, "what a pleasant journey Nereiðr and what gentle folk the dwarfs are" she said in a voice louder than normal. Nereiðr said nothing but continued to walk, a smile playing on his face and as they strode across ranks of workmen, the whistles and compliments kept coming Natasha's way. "I'll forgo all the lips I've kissed for the chance of pressing my lips against hers" whispered a voice from nowhere. "Well" said Natasha to herself this was certainly the place to be for a lady. Granted in didn't have the luxuries of a palace and there were no maids and servants to run around catering to her every whim but the compliments she received more than made up for it.

"And when she sighs the world sighed with her and when smiled the world smiled with her" …. "Her hair was long; a sweet smelling strawberry blonde with luscious lashes that covered eyes that were bluer than the ocean's tide". The dwarfs continued singing her praises and the princess thought that it was only proper than she said a few words to them. So as the pair walked past the workers the "angel of morn" as the dwarfs called her repeatedly said "thank you" in the sweetest voice she could muster.

"Like they elves, dwarfs, are magical creatures" said Nereiðr. Natasha listened keenly to what he had to say. "They have the ability to see through mortal facades and they can tell if a person's soul is pure or tainted". Natasha smiled at what was undoubtedly a compliment and said "They appear to be the noblest of creatures with the highest integrity" she said her voice full of confidence boosted by the unanticipated flow of compliments that unexpectedly came surging her way.

They reached another opening and they entered a passage that split into two different paths. "The trail on the left will take us to the caverns below, while the trail on the right will take us to the rich ore mines that are being excavated". "You will have to say goodbye to your dear friends" little one said the elf. Natasha looked slightly disappointed, the compliments had come to an end all too soon but no matter, she decided. She'll return at a later time armed with a basket filled with sandwiches. The wise elf read her thoughts and said "Like elves they are vegetarians but the preferred sandwiches made from mushrooms and they had a special preference for salted cheese".

That was easy enough to make and it had been sometime since she had been anywhere near a kitchen with the exception of camp fires and even then she hadn't done any cooking. A general could hardly be expected to toil away at a makeshift stove preparing meals for hundreds of men. Often however it was a matter of living off dried rations usually fruits enriched with nutrients. For months it had made been her only source of sustenance.

The path sloped downwards and as they ventured further deeper into the caverns she felt like she could hear the chorus of the seas. Despite being surrounded by enclosed walls she had the feeling of walking under the infinite sky, on the soft, sultry sand of a golden beach and the incoherent sounds that filled her ears were similar to the restless noise made by boisterous waves.

It was a magical place and they soon found themselves in an underground grotto. Its walls and towers appeared to overlook a garden of flowers and they were trapped in a magical web of dazzling colors. The sounds of the waves were soon replaced by that of singing of birds, ringing out from all corners of the subterranean dwelling accompanied by the fragrance of sweet smelling roses. She looked ahead at the elf that lead the way and the surface of his skin started to glow incandescently with each step that he took. A discreet breeze blew from ahead and his white silken robes fluttered to the wind. Soon he began to emit a bright white light, like that of a shining star.

She looked down at the palms of her hands and like the skin on Nereiðr's body her palms had assumed a solar glow. She too was transforming and it dawned on her that the invisible armor that she had on her presence was becoming more apparent as they drew closer to the lair of the dragon mages. She was certain that it was the magic of Dragos that precipitated the transformation. Everything here was filled with his magic.

The light within the cavern increased growing brighter with each passing second. It was like she was walking towards the sun. She sped up and reached out to grab Nereiðr's arm. She felt comforted by the touch of his hand as the light before them grew increasingly fluorescent. The visions that flashed before her appeared slower than normal like she was trapped in a dream. The clock ticked at a slower pace and she felt herself being magnetically pulled towards a bright luminous light. "We are approaching the lair of the dragon mages" said Nereiðr.

Her consciousness was adrift and she felt like she was travelling to another world. The air around her glittered and glimmered with solar dust and she could make out a chamber. In it there were five hooded elves seated on crimson cushions "Dragon mages" whispered Nereiðr in her ear. They were seated in a circle, legs crossed on the cushions, their minds asleep, sharing the transcendental slumber of the wind-drifter. She felt the touch of a gentle wind. "The wind that embraces you is the solar wind. Dragos favors you my child" said Nereiðr.

Natasha was overwhelmed and remained silent, awestruck by what she was experiencing. "Let us wait for the moment to pass" said the elf. The waited patiently for what seemed like ages for the ambiance to return to normal. It soon passed and they were once again in the realm of the elves. She looked around and outside the stone crafted chamber she could see elves, dressed in green and gold, in the colors of the sacred forest, plodding along. Her eyes strayed around the room taking in as much as they could when she spotted a lady walking towards her, her hair as golden as the rays of the mortal sun, slightly taller than Natasha but otherwise of similar bodily proportions.

The grotto looked more like a home than a subterranean dwelling. With the exception of the chamber; everything else looked the norm. The elf with the golden hair was dressed in robes of flowing silk. She walked casually up to the pair and formally greeted the elf elder. "Welcome Nereiðr" she said before pointing her finger at Natasha and asking Nereiðr "who is your little friend?" "This is Natasha, Princess of Mirkash" said Nereiðr making the appropriate introductions. "Ah, the lady with the armor of the sun" she said. Natasha looked surprised. "You're famous little one" said the elf with the golden hair looking directly at the young lady. The princess looked slightly disconcerted. "Come princess" she said leading the way. "We have been expecting you for years".

"I am Runa of the Vale, Master Mage of the Dragon Mages" she introduced herself. "What you see around you is the abode of the dragon mages. We are a school, small and

74

secluded and almost all but forgotten". "We record all the findings and discoveries made by the dragon mages when they shared the mind of the dragons and we store them for posterity" she continued. Natasha nodded her head and listened keenly.

"There are only five dragons born of this world, one of each kind". We believe that all the dragons are in some way connected to the eternal consciousness of Dragos, the solar dragon. Thus far none of the mages have yet ventured close enough to grasp the complexities of his nature".

"And you believe that I'm the one that has been chosen to do so" added Natasha without waiting for Runa to continue. The Master Mage nodded her head. "It has to be you because you are gifted with the armor of the sun. It not only shields you from mortal weapons, it also shields you from the extreme heat of the sun and you among all mortals will be able to approach the core of the sun".

"Likewise you'll be able to approach Dragos, who burns with the effulgence of a billion suns and yet not be fazed by the intolerable heat". Natasha listened in silence.

"In some ways you are lucky because the choice of dragons has been made for you. The wind-drifter is the only dragon that remains in the known world. The others have drifted to other worlds but they may return in time. The dragon mages who have been adjoined to the respective dragons are carefully monitoring the progress of the dragons in this and other worlds".

"The wind-drifter is the most placid of the dragons and the most spiritual of all the children of Dragos. He is more attuned to incorporeal exploits and he rarely troubles himself with material contemplations. He is much the philosopher and I dare say you will grow to love him" continued Runa.

"But as I understand it the dragon has already been adjoined to five different mages" the princess unable to contain herself any longer interjected. "How will I be able to share the consciousness of a dragon that has already been linked to the consciousness of others?" she asked. "A pertinent questions your highness" said Nereiðr.

Runa paused before she replied. "It is done by transferring the consciousness of the dragon mages to you. Remember princess that the consciousness of all creation, all life, all objects, animate and inanimate is linked to the super-consciousness or the consciousness of the Brahmatma. I will aid you in your attempt to access the consciousness or the memories of the wind-drifter".

"I as Master Mage share the consciousness of all the five dragons. I will transfer the memories and recollections of the wind-drifter to you and once your consciousness has been fused with that of the wind-drifter, you will be the sole dragon mage responsible for the dragon and the present mages will disengage from having any further contact with it" she added.

"But won't the wind-drifter be aware that the current mages have withdrawn and that a new consciousness has been melded with its own?" asked the princess. Runa smiled "No doubt" she said. "The consciousness of all dragon kind is linked to Dragos and it is simply a matter of obtaining his consent". "Thus far we know that he approves of you and that is all that matters" she added.

She led Natasha to a room and the princess was made to lie down on a bed of white velvet and covered with a blanket made of the purest and softest wool. The temperature in the room was slowly reduced to below the norm and the air grew gradually colder.

The master mage then handed the princess a small beaker which contained a small amount of liquid that looked very much like egg white. "Please drink it down" she said. The princess did as she was told and discovered that the liquid tasted very much like sparkling wine only thicker.

She handed the beaker back to a smiling Runa who patiently stood beside her bed. The princess was then made to listen to the soothing voice of the master mage as she gently repeated an ancient mantra and coaxed the princess into sleep. The sleep that the princess was under was known as induced sleep or sleep that is the result of other than normal factors. The senses are gently persuaded to cease functioning and the rate of the heart beat is gradually reduced in stages.

The transfer was initiated once the princess had regressed into a state of deep meditative slumber and the conscious mind ceased to be active and the subconscious mind swung into action. Runa then reached out with her mind and accessed the collective memory of the super consciousness, a vast warehouse or storage facility that stored the memories of all creation. She had to navigate through an extensive labyrinth to search for the princess's consciousness. It was by no means an easy task but she soon found it.

The transfer was normally simplified if there was an emotional bond that linked both the minds. Emotions strengthened the nexus between two minds and when this link or bond is in place it became easier to transfer the consciousness or share the thoughts between two people. Once she had located Natasha's consciousness the master mage began to meld her mind with that of the princess and started transferring the memories that were relevant to the wind-drifter to Natasha's consciousness from her own.

Natasha's inner vision was first blanketed by a vast emptiness before she saw a light flash before her eyes followed by a burst that instantly took her to another constellation and to a world that was infinitely larger than theirs. A world that was lighted by two suns that blazed on opposite sides, Gamma and Draconis. Right between them, smack in the middle, was the planet Draco Prime, home of the dragons and ruled my Dragos supreme leader and god personified of dragon kind.

Like Natasha dragons were solar entities, children of the sun, who breathed and bathed in the munificent rays of the sun. It was a planet with skies, water, earth and greenery. Parts of it were so hot that it contained pools of molten lava.

The dragon race was the first to occupy the planet. Dragos was the primordial dragon and upon him was bestowed the title solar dragon. Dragos divided the kingdom between his five children. The first was the pale dragon and to him Dragos granted dominion of the skies and all things relating to aether, spirits and religion. His second child was the blue dragon and to him Dragos granted dominion over waters and all things that existed on and beneath water. To his third child the earth dragon he granted dominion of the earth and all things that existed on and beneath the earth. To his fourth child the wind dragon who was also known as the frost dragon, he granted dominion over the winds, the polar caps and all things made of ice and to his last child the red dragon that reveled in pits of molten lava, he granted dominion over fires, volcanoes and all things that bellow in the bellies and craters of mountains. The red dragon was the fieriest of all his five children.

Natasha's consciousness quickly sifted through the memories of the wind-drifter. The dragons and their hatchlings existed in peace and serenity for eons until the arrival of the serpent-eels, slimy, slithery creatures of darkness that mysteriously appeared out of the blue, falling like rain from the skies. They crept and crawled into the dragon lairs and fed on the yoke of dragon eggs. The serpent-eels multiplied in no time and infested the land in numbers. Their slippery treachery angered Dragos, God of Dragon Lore, and he made the twin suns Gamma and Draconis expand to dimensions a thousand times their normal size.

The scorching heat that resulted from the expansion of the dual suns incinerated the serpent dragons and the feeders beasts on the planet within the blink of an eye. The dragons were forced to flee to other planets in order to avoid starvation. In time Dragos returned Gamma and Draconis to their normal size but by then no life remained on the planet.

The eggs that were salvaged were encased in meteorites and hurled into space and one of the egg laden meteorites landed on the outskirts of the sacred forest. The eggs arrived at a time when the world was rife with white magic and at a time when the earth burgeoned with magical creatures. The eggs in the rock covered casing were discovered by Runa.

Natasha gasped when she realized the age of the master mage. She appeared before her in the dreamlike vision that accompanied the transfer, seated astride a winged unicorn, its coat glimmering in snow white splendor, amidst puffy clouds and its horn glistened and glimmered in the light of the sun. He was by far the most majestic animal she had ever seen, his eyes shimmering with the surface blue of the ocean. His unstained coat clung softly his body and Runa hung on to his pure ivory mane while his tail blew gently in the wind, as the pair hopped from one cloud to another.

She spotted the meteorite nestled in the middle of a lavender bush, wedged in a shallow crater and guided the unicorn to a landing close beside it. Runa jumped off the unicorn and walked over to the meteorite. She reached out to touch the surface of the rock and the moment it felt her touch, the rock split open to reveal five eggs each the size of a full grown dwarf. Taken aback the princess sent her unicorn, Sir Valiant back to beckon for help and soon Nereiðr arrived with a team of elves and dwarfs on horse carts. The eggs were carefully loaded on the back of the carts and taken to Mount Kieddoaivi. There they were transported through passages to the underground caverns and incubated in a hot volcanic pool.

Runa knew exactly what to do without being told, which Natasha found curious. She made a mental note to ask her about it when the situation permitted.

She saw the dragon mages that were adjoined to the wind-drifter in their youth. Five elven maidens no older than eighteen with hair the color of golden straw and eyes as blue as sapphire. Together with Runa, they shared the earliest memories of the wind-drifter.

In time she began to feel the presence of the dragon. The infant dragon had emotions like that of a child and as soon as it hatched it started to look around for a matron and not being able to find one, it turned to Dragos, who guided it by thought. If the Supreme Dragon felt Natasha intruding on the wind-drifter's memories, he said or did nothing. Instead Dragos let her probe further while the wind-drifter continued with its transcendental slumber.

Dragons fed only on meat which Runa purchased from mortal butchers. Soon bushels of meat were carted from butchers located in villages close to the fringes of the sacred forest and carted to the foot of the Kieddoaivi. The dragon mages who shared the dragon's consciousness over time developed a craving for meat and shared the dragon's appetite.

The dragon grew up in no time and the wind-drifter soon consumed carts of roast sheep and lamb but fortunately it fed only once a month and whiled the rest of the month away in slumber unless there was some pressing matter that the dragon mages wanted attended to.

The dragon spirit had the ability to separate from the soul at will and while the physical dragon was asleep the spiritual aspect of the dragon travelled vast distances in search of knowledge. Dragons had a craving for knowledge and it was based on the Supreme Dragon's prime directive that all dragons were to acquire as much knowledge as possible. He in turn accessed the knowledge from the collective consciousness that he shared with them. In this manner Dragos kept tabs on the universe.

Natasha IX

The wind drifter looked like a big lizard with a pair of bat wings on the sides of its body. Its head was decorated with a set of horns and it had spikes on its neck and on its tail which culminated in a rock hard spade.

It had a broad chest with wings that spurted from miniature shoulders just below the chest. The dragon had two pairs of legs, the former doubled up as arms. Instead of fingers it had five sharp talons on each of its four feet.

Its belly was located between the first pair of feet and the second pair of feet. The infant wind-drifted released tiny puffs of smokes from its nostrils every time it breathed that drifted upwards to the roof of the cave. It was a pretty creature and Natasha like Runa felt like a proud mother.

Within a month the dragon had quadrupled in size and Runa chaperoned it out of the cave. The wind-drifter was delighted at the sight of the sun and flapped its wing trying to take off. Its first flight was nothing short of a total disaster and it crashed after travelling a few cubits.

Dragons were diligent creatures and the wind drifter despite the initial failures, kept trying. Within the space of a few days it had managed to get the hang of flying in the air, after repeatedly crashing into trees.

Takeoffs and landings were its greatest flaws during its early trials but it soon mastered it and eventually acquired the ability to fly higher and higher into the clouds. The dragon's sole destination was the sun. Being a solar entity the child of Dragos kept wanting to get as close to the sun as possible.

Eventually it managed to come to terms with the intricacies of flight and managed to grasp the subtle nuances of being a dragon. After months of being allowed to fly on its own, Runa latched on to its back and went for a ride. She grabbed on to the spike close to the base of the neck. The spikes on the dragon's neck resembled ivory tusks and were easy to hold on to. The dragon and the master mage spoke only with the mind and Runa guided the wind-drifter on the path that it wanted the dragon to take.

The pair spent hours in the sky while the dragon mages withdrew to cozy grottos located in the subterranean caverns. The five female elves never again saw the light of day and remained within the confines of the grotto sharing the consciousness of the dragon.

Runa devoted her time to all the five dragons while the mages concerned themselves only with the individual dragons that were in their care. After the initial stages of bonding the master mage left the day to day care of the dragons in the hands of the mages. Those were the early days during which they shared only joy and laughter and enjoyed the pleasures of learning but soon all that was about to change and dark clouds unexpectedly loomed ominously over the horizon.

The clouds milled around and eventually grew so large that they blocked the sun. The dragons grew restless and tossed and turned in their sleep. The lack of sunlight troubled them and they refused to stay calm. The mages had a difficult time trying to pacify them. As the days progressed the dark clouds broke and pelted the land with rain and hail that destroyed homes and crops aided by strong gusts of unholy winds that blew at hurricane speeds. The temperatures began to plummet and sleet and snow covered the fields. It was like the start of another ice age.

Distant volcanoes began to churn and from their bellies molten lava burst forth and formed streams of liquid that reduced the valleys below to smoldering ashes. Even the frost dragon grew uneasy and the white magic that protected the earth started to falter.

After what seemed like months of rain and hail that had washed away fertile lands the forces of Ahriman gathered. They banded together from distant worlds and descended from the skies falling to the ground in hordes.

The fallen as they were called were twisted and deformed and they were grotesquely disfigured in appearance. Their eyes burnt with rage and they went instantly on a killing spree. Soon the rivers of the known world were flowing not with water but with blood. The war that followed ravaged and devastated the known world leaving in its wake a sordid tale of death and misery.

Images retained in the memories of Dragos came flooding through and Natasha could see the similarities between the pandemic evil that had suddenly and unexpectedly descended unto the known world and the serpent-eels that had devastated Draco Prime.

The dragons stood with the elven race and inflicted severe casualties on the demonic invaders but even with their help the elf population was reduced by half. To make matters worse, the twisted priests of Ahriman managed to introduce new variants into the population. Dark elves were but one of the unholy species that had endured since the battle before time and had become a permanent albeit little known feature.

Captured elves were forced to conjugate with demons and the cohesive interaction resulted in the birth of dark elves who were so perverse by nature and design that the sun destroyed them on sight. The dragons unleashed torrents of flame reducing the abominations to ashes but they survived lurking in dark unknown woods and the deep subterranean caves of the mortal world.

By the end of the war the elven population was reduced by half and what remained of the elves withdrew into the folds of forests like the sacred forest that were located in secluded and isolated locations around the known world. The forests were shrouded by magic so intricate that it was accessible only to the highest ranking members of the Order of Dawn.

In the aftermath of the mammoth battle four of the dragons left for other worlds in order to expand their knowledge while the wind-drifter relocated to occupy the peaks of a distant mountain and there it went into deep meditation in search of spiritual rectitude.

Of all the dragons from the known world it was the most spiritual and sought reprieve from the carnage that it had caused during the great battle. Natasha could sense that the dragon felt no remorse for dragons had a deeply ingrained sense of right and wrong and the wind-drifter knew that by diminishing Ahriman's strengths it had saved the lives of countless mortals, magical creatures and other celestial beings but despite that it chose to seek redemption.

Its consciousness was locked away on a planet close to the sun and it lolled in the heat of the giant flamboyant sun that never ceased to flare. It was a planet without day and night with only the unyielding light of the yellow sun which continuously set its surface alight.

Natasha unlike the dragon mages who shared the consciousness of the wind-drifter could transport herself to the planet's surface because of the armor that was gifted to her at birth. She teleported herself via the dragon's consciousness and was soon on the planet's surface.

She could sense the wind drifter smile as her feet gingerly touched the arid ground and she felt its breath on her. She could hear its thoughts - a voice inside her head said silently, in a soft soothing voice, "you're on the planet of the Goddess that ushers in the morn, Dawn, the darling of the Adityas and the Mitras. Like us she too is a solar entity dear Natasha" - it was the voice of the wind-drifter. The voice disappeared as quickly as it had come.

Natasha thought over what she had just heard, so this was the home planet of Dawn of the race of Gods, the daughter of Aditi, one the loveliest women to ever grace the known world - the goddess who guided her maidens to victory. The intense heat had no effect on the princess and her perceptions were keener than normal. She moved around and her consciousness moved faster than her mortal feet could carry her. She felt a comforting wind; it was the breath of the wind-drifter. She realized that she wasn't mothering the dragon anymore. If anything it was the dragon that was mothering her.

Their minds were merging and they were becoming a single entity in soul and spirit. The dragon was helping her through the process. In occurred to her that she may never awake from the sleep that she was in but that didn't seem to matter. She could see herself lying on the soft cushioned bed. The master mage was no longer by her side and she was on her own. Her skin was no longer pale but a radiant solar white. It was shining and shimmering and glowed in a magical manner. "You share the gift of Dragos, solar child" said the wind-drifter. Natasha bowed her head in humility.

She moved through the planet, it had a name that was unpronounceable in the mortal tongue. Even the wind-drifter had difficulties with it and hence the pair referred to it only as the Planet of Dawn. Natasha travelled vast distances in a matter of seconds and scoured the surface of the planet. While she possessed all her physical and mental capacities and capabilities, she was in reality a light no bigger than the size of a thumb. The planet was uninhabited but it was not without constructions. Dawn herself lived here and there were huge citadels sculpted from pure granite inlaid with gold reinforced by the unrepentant heat.

She stepped into the largest citadel and she entered through an open doorway onto a corridor. The heat disappeared instantly. "You've entered the Palace of Dawn" said the wind-drifter. "Thank you" said Natasha uttering her first words to the dragon. The wind-drifter said nothing but merely let out a cheery grunt that echoed discreetly in her head. She felt a soothing breeze caress the skin on her body. She looked up at a roof that was so high that all she could see above was a vast empty space.

She looked around and there were a collection of objects some which she recognized as objects from the known world and others that she did not recognize and were not of her world. She saw a sculpture that stood at least twenty cubits high, chiseled from a single block of diamond, dressed in solar armor. Her hair was long and golden and a plaited crown decorated her head.

Her features were regal and majestic, oozing immeasurable power. "Behold the Empress of the Morn - Dawn" said the wind-drifter. Contrary to mortal perceptions Dawn looked very much like a warrior goddess and very unlike the normal depictions that portrayed her as a frail maiden. She wielded a sword in her right hand and a larger circular shield on her left. The face of her shield was engraved with the bright face of the sun.

She caught the glint of light in the corner of her eye and she turned her head to try and discover its origins. Hanging in front of her was a sword almost three cubits in length from hilt to toe made of a yellowish metal that shinned and shimmered like gold but she suspected that it was made from a far more superior metal and infinitely more valuable than mortal gold. "The Sword of Dawn" said the wind-drifter. "Move towards it Natasha" said the dragon gently and the princess obeyed. She reached out and touched the handle of the sword tentatively with her hand.

She felt a sudden surge of energy rush through her veins that immediately sent her heart thumping. She wrapped her hand around the hilt of the sword and it felt warm and welcoming. She lifted the sword with its sheath intact from the wall it clung to and discovered that there were straps fastened to the cover that allowed her to latch the sword onto her back. She slipped her arms through the straps and attached the sword to her back in the manner of a warrior priestess. As she did so a little globe appeared from nowhere. It gradually increased in size until it manifested into a full grown woman dressed in silken white robes her features identical to the sculpted figure that she had just seen moments ago.

The princess went down on one knee and knelt before the Empress of the Morn who held in her outstretched hand a round shield and impressed on its face was the head of a fiery golden-red dragon. "A gift dear Natasha from the solar dragon Dragos" she said softly to the young princess. "Take it Natasha, take it" urged the wind-drifter from nowhere. Natasha accepted the gift and Dawn smiled. "Goodbye for now, my dear princess" she said and the orb decreased in size before the Goddess disappeared.

She was moving again and she felt herself drifting through space, past stars and constellations before she found herself in the underground grotto. She awoke from sleep only to find the five dragon mages standing by her bedside. She tried to get up but had difficulty getting on to her feet. She felt slightly disorientated and fell back into bed. "Easy little one" she heard a sweet gentle voice speak to her. It was one of the hooded mages. "It takes some time for the body to return to normality after it had been in transcendental sleep" the mage continued. "You are unlike the rest of us" said another voice. "You can move about while sharing the consciousness of the wind-drifter". "You're special little one".

She lay in bed for at least a day slipping in and out of sleep before she got up. Natasha looked at herself in the mirror and looked exactly like she did in her vision. Her skin was no longer pale but had instead assumed the solar hue of Dragos. She could see the straps of the sword visibly attached to her shoulders. "You are now a dragon mage" said a familiar voice from behind. Natasha turned and saw Runa whose face was beaming with a smile.

"In time you will assume my role" she added. Natasha looked slightly disconcerted. "It is not my intention to be master mage" said the princess deferentially. "It is your destiny child, don't fight it" consoled Runa gently.

Natasha remained silent. She avoided looking into the eyes of the master mage and shifted her attention to the covers of her bed. She couldn't help but wonder what was to become of Runa. On her bed she saw the shield of Dragos. Uncertain, she reached for the hilt of the sword that was strapped to her back and wrapped her fingers around the handle for comfort. Not wanting to draw the sword from its sheath, she let it remain.

She turned her attention to the mirror and looked at herself again. Every inch of her body was covered with the solar armor including her face which was shielded with a glowing mask.

She turned to Runa and asked "How do I remove it?". "You merely wish it away" replied Runa "and if you want it back on, you simply wish it back". "It is all done by thought" she explained. Natasha tried it and true enough her armor disappeared. "I'm now part dragon aren't I?" she asked.

Runa nodded her head. "In time you'll be a full dragon and lose all semblance of mortality" she continued. "I'm sorry princess" said Runa. "Oh Runa don't be, I'm happy to be a dragon". "No creature in existence has given me so much joy" Natasha said quickly. The wind-drifter let out a loud guffaw. "Well spoken princess, well spoken" it said.

Natasha wished her armor back on and it reappeared instantly. If the truth be told she rather liked it and for the first time since she'd been gifted with the armor she felt invincible. She spoke silently to the wind-drifter. They spoke in thought. "Are you still asleep" she asked. "I am" replied the dragon. "Well isn't it time to wake up?" she asked. The wind-drifter sounded amused. "Not yet little solar dragon, please let me rest a little longer". "You'll be the first to known when I'm awake because I'll be famished and you'll feel hunger like never before" it said.

"Don't worry, I'll find us a nice flock of sheep to feast on" she replied with a gentle laugh and the wind-drifter chuckled in reply. "Nothing like roasting it" added the dragon. A range of recipes suddenly flooded through both their minds and Natasha felt her mouth watering. Boiled mutton, braised mutton, barbecued mutton dripped in scintillating sauces. It was just too much to resist. She realized that she had begun to abhor the vegan diet that she was so used to.

Natasha bid her mentor Runa goodbye and made her way out of the grotto, holding her shield in her left hand, she strode back onto the passage that had brought her there. As soon as did so an invisible door softly closed behind her. She found Nereiðr waiting for her. He bowed his head as soon as he saw her and said "welcome Natasha Dragana".... "Natasha Dragana" .... the princess thought over her new name and decided that she rather liked it.

She walked back with Nereiðr to the mouth of the cave and on their way back, they passed the dwarf workmen again. Instead of being greeted by flattering whistles they were ushered with low bowed heads and hushed whispers.

"There goes the Empress" said a dwarf. "Natasha Dragana" said another. "What a lovely Empress she is" added a third voice. Natasha made up her mind. She definitely liked the dwarfs.

It was noon when they stepped out of the cave and Natasha felt the warmth of the sun beating down on her.

She relished every drop of sunlight that touched her skin. She savored the solar nectar and understood why the wind-drifter sought to be closer to the sun. Dragons not only fed on food but also on sunlight.

Natasha X

On the journey back they had a chance to discuss the ongoing war in Lamunia. "I feel that it is only appropriate to inform you that the situation on the battle front has deteriorated somewhat" said Nereiðr. "Oh??" inquired Natasha. Despite the precarious nature of the war, Natasha had become so engrossed with the unexpected transition and all thoughts of the invaders had been pushed to the back of her mind. She wondered if Amesha Spenta would be displeased but soon dismissed the notion.

The God King even if he was vexed with her actions or inactions would be pleased with a victory and she intended to give him just that.

"It is time to wake up the wind-drifter" she said with a touch of authority. "Precisely Natasha Dragana" said Nereiðr. Natasha reached out with her consciousness and came in contact with her other half, who coincidentally had decided to go on a spiritual journey of its own while the empress was preoccupied with Runa and Nereiðr.

Her consciousness breached vast distances in a matter of seconds. She drifted through constellations and soon found herself on Orion the hunter, on a planet that was lit by four red giants, one on each direction of the compass. It was extremely hot and the surface of the planet was nothing more than streams of molten lava. The sky had a yellowish-reddish tinge that lingered without respite over the horizon. The planet was a furnace that was neither hospitable nor habitable.

She found the dragon sprawled away in the rigorous heat. "My sibling the red dragon loves it here" said the wind-drifter, "as do I". Natasha felt the extreme heat touch her armor and she was instantly rejuvenated and reinvigorated. She felt the uncontrollable compulsion to go nearer to the red giant and the dragon encouraged her. "Go on Empress" said the wind-drifter and Natasha unable to resist any longer, urged her consciousness closer to the red giant.

As she got nearer to the sun she felt heat waves, winds travelling at incredible speeds and moving at an indefinable velocity, come at her from all directions. She felt more alive than ever and she found herself gliding around the star. It was like a game and she travelled around the red giant propelled by the solar winds. The wind drifter chuckled, "I love this game" it said. "I think I will join you" and within seconds she saw her other half. It was a handsome creature, the prettiest dragon in existence.

The scales on its body were smooth and lithe and its face was simply divine. "Stretch your wings my love" she said and the wind drifted complied. The giant bat wings stretched for almost one hundred and thirty cubits from tip to tip. Natasha felt the urge to sit on its back. "Come Empress" invited the dragon and Natasha obliged moving closer to the wind-drifter eventually seating herself on its back. It was an incredible feeling and she no longer felt the desire to move. She grabbed hold of the dragon's spike that was closest to her and like Runa before her guided it instinctively with her mind towards the center of the red giant.

The dragon flapped its wings and in one swift motion hurled itself at the core of the red giant. As they moved closer she felt a surge of power and her armor began to glow incandescently emanating the brilliance of a star.

The outer core of the red giant comprised of waves of gases that continuously slammed against each other at incredible speeds and with unmitigated force. It was exhilarating. Every gush, every swell sent chimes of ecstasy that swept through her body like unquenchable flames of desire. As the wind-drifter drew closer to the blazing inferno the surges grew more intense.

"You're becoming a dragon Empress" said the wind-drifter. Natasha said nothing, unable to contain her joy. She felt incredible power and as the pair breached the crust and reached the mantle, the Empress began to glow like a sun, increasing in radiance as the approached the inner core.

The dragon hurled itself at the core of the sun and the pair breezed right through it. By the time they reached the other side the wind- drifter was wide awake. She heard the voice of Nereiðr yell out from somewhere. "Caution, Natasha Dragana, caution, you have awakened the wind-drifter" but Natasha didn't feel like being cautious. If anything she felt like being the exact opposite and recklessly rode away on the dragon's back. She heard Nereiðr sigh.

She suddenly felt hunger pangs, pure unadulterated hunger unlike anything she had ever felt before. They were thinking in unison, the wind-drifter and the empress. "Food" she yelled out aloud and the wind-drifter agreed. They flew at incredible speeds and flashed past stars and constellations.

They streamed through galaxies in a matter of minutes propelled by their consciousness and soon found themselves on a planet much like that of the known world with green pastures. The dragon spotted a herd of sheep grazing in the meadow under the watchful eye of a shepherd.

With outstretched wings, the wind-drifter swooped down and by so doing temporarily blocked the light that the planet's sole sun emitted. The shepherd looked up to see what had caused the unexpected eclipse and realizing that it was a dragon, he yelled out as loudly as he could "dragon!!" "dragon!!" trying to alert anyone who was close by and ran for cover. "How would you like your meat dear Empress" the dragon inquired.

"Medium rare, please" she replied and the dragon obliged. It inhaled, holding its breath for a second before letting out a torrent of temperate flame that had the meat cooked in a matter of seconds. "Sheep and lamb roast Empress" said the dragon before it landed next to the charred remains. Natasha jumped off its back and tore the leg off the roasted carcass that was closest to her and bit into it.

The meat tasted delectable and the Empress savored every bite. Before she realized it she had guzzled down the whole lamb. She looked around only to realize that the wind-drifter had polished off the whole flock. "More?" asked the dragon and the Empress nodded. There was distant sound and it was another sigh.

They fed through the day devouring almost half the meat in a kingdom located above a tall scraggly cliff overlooking a vast sea with towered castles spread across the interior before they made their way back to the sacred forest in search of Nereiðr.

They found him seated on a slab of rock close to the foot of the mountain where Natasha had left him. The elf had spotted them coming and waved his hands at them eagerly.

Natasha tried to make sense of how she had covered such vast distances at such incredibly short spans of time and the dragon explained. "You have the ability Empress, like all dragons, to transport yourself to any location that is visible to your consciousness". "In mortal terms it is called astral projection or the ability to journey to any location that is stored in the mind. It is no secret that dragons inherit the memories of their ancestors at birth and that includes all the places their predecessors had visited".

The dragon landed close to the foot of the mountain and Natasha clambered off the Dragon's back. "Welcome back Natasha Dragana" said the elf. He paused before he continued "I realize you're an Empress now but I would appreciate some notice before you sped off the next time" said Nereiðr. "Oh I'm so sorry" said the princess trying to think of an explanation. The wind-drifter quickly intervened on her behalf and said "She's a dragon now Nereiðr" it said solemnly. "That explains it then does it?" asked the elf. The dragon chuckled in reply while the Empress remained silent. "Come now Nereiðr it is only to be expected" said the Dragon. "I suppose it is" said the elf with feigned resignation.

"I think it is time that you returned to the battle front Natasha" said Nereiðr or all might be lost". "Your troops are not faring well" and "it's been years since you left them" he said. Natasha looked puzzled "Years??" "I've only been here for a few days, Nereiðr, a week at most" she said surprised, uncertain if the elf was pulling her leg.

"Nay child" said the elf. You've been here for five years". "You lost all track of time while you were in transcendental sleep" he said. Natasha looked perplexed and was suddenly overcome by concern "what of my men?" she asked. "They survive but barely". "You have at best, five thousand men left" he continued. Natasha's face hardened. "And the rest?" she asked. "They took no prisoners" he replied calmly.

Under normal circumstances the princess would have been reduced to tears but that was not the case this time and she felt a sudden surge of anger flood through her veins reaching every nook and cranny in her body. Every fiber in her body began to glow with anger emitting the all too familiar solar hue. Dragon rage it was called and her other half the wind-drifter grew increasingly restless, its head tossing and turning as it let out torrents of flame from its nostrils aimed at the sky.

"Calm down child" Nereiðr tried to console her but it was easier said than done. Dragons were quick to anger and once their temper had been set alight it could not be smothered or soothed with words. There was a glint of steel in her eyes, "to battle" she yelled. The wind-drifter nodded its head, dragon rage rushing to every corner of its body.

<hr />

Captain Azardokht studied the line, her eyes looking for signs of weakness that might force her archers to break but she couldn't find any. Captain Irdeh had stationed her horse lancers on the hill to the left and Captain Zavareh had his men positioned just behind the archers to give them time to escape after they had released their arrows.

The east was defended by what remained of the one hundred and seventy four thousand strong alliance that had been sent to defend Lamunia including the subsequent replacements and reinforcements. It was without doubt a final stand and their chances of winning were slim to say the least. Victory was within Azag's grasp. Lamunia for all intense and purposes had fallen.

They had fought valiantly for five years following the sudden disappearance of the princess and general who was chosen to lead them. She had mysteriously vanished during a routine leave of absence that was scheduled to last for no longer than a fortnight.

While there was no concrete evidence connecting her disappearance to Azag but the camp was rife with rumors. According to some rather dubious informers the princess had been kidnapped and taken to one of the central kingdoms. Other unsubstantiated sources suggested that the princess had fallen under an evil spell and was now a member of Azag's inner circle. If that wasn't enough there was a third rumor that declared that Hawk's Nest itself was behind her disappearance. Because of her growing popularity she had become a threat to Amesha Spenta and by continuously asking for prisoners of war to be rehabilitated instead of executed, she had incurred the wrath of the God King. Despite repeated attempts to confirm these rumors Hawk's Nest chose to remain silent on the matter which only served to add fuel to the fire.

In her absence the mantle of leadership had passed on to the most senior member of the team, Captain Zavareh of the Imperial Guards. The esteemed Captain had repeatedly requested for fresh troops to be sent to bolster the defenses of Lamunia but Hawk's Nest and Amesha Spenta had refused. With the exception of regular supplies the God King hadn't helped in any other way. Maybe it was their destiny to perish in the battlefields of Southern Lamunia.

Captain Golnaz awoke at dawn that morning. Azag's troops were closing in and would soon be upon them. It was most likely her last day on earth. She lamented the loss of the battle implements that she had so meticulously designed and so carefully constructed but it was unavoidable. They might have stood a chance if the mechanisms that she had assembled were in position but sadly that was not to be.

The smell of blood and grime drifted through the air and she could hear the distant drum of boots and horseshoes treading against the hard ground. She caught sight of a cloud of dust rising up against the skyline in the light of the early sun.

She knelt and gazed at the rising sun, an embodiment of the virtues of Asha and ablaze with the light of Athra. Just as she was about to wish for a speedy death, for she saw no other way out she saw a tiny bloat in the middle of the solar disc. It grew larger by the second and she gasped .... it wasn't possible but there it was right in front of her - a dragon its pale scales unmistakable in the backdrop of the golden sun. There was something on its back. She peered at the object and as improbable as it was, her keen eyes told her that it was an armored rider.

The camp was suddenly abuzz and every soldier turned his or her attention to watch the dragon, one of the many wonders of creation, and in so doing abandoned their respective posts. For a moment all thoughts of Azag and the approaching men were forgotten and their attentions were turned to the winged object in the sky that blotted out the sun as it approached and hovered briefly over them. Some fell to their knees in prayer. It was infinitely better to be killed by a dragon than to be diced to death by the flashing swords of Azag's men.

Then rather unexpectedly the silhouette turned and moved north and rays of sunlight came filtering through once again. Golnaz, Azardokth and Zavareh watched as the dragon faded away over the horizon and just as they thought it was about to disappear they saw torrents of flames shoot down from the sky like comets and clouds of smoke rose up in the air soon after accompanied by the stench of charred flesh.

Within minutes reports came streaming through. "The dragon is attacking Azag's men" was all that Golnaz heard before she stopped listening. She leapt with joy, elated. It was all over within minutes and the long arduous battle that had lasted years had finally come to an end. Azag and his men were reduced to smoldering ashes and Lamunia was saved, temporarily at least. The dragon after reducing the enemy to cinders flew towards the sun together with its mysterious rider and eventually disappeared into the large solar disc.

Epilogue

A hooded priest made his way into the carpeted hall of the throne room in Hawk's Nest. Ensconced on the seat of infinite power was the God King, Amesha Spenta. The hooded priest bowed in front of the tall, lanky man, who sat nonchalantly on the throne. He waved his hand signaling for the priest to speak. "It is done my lord, Azag walks no longer in the world of the living" he said. The God King smiled and stroked the hair on the hilt of his sword as it nestled on his lap. Chandi was pleased and she whispered so in his ear. "And what of the princess?" he asked. "She is now a dragon mage, as you wished my lord" the priest answered. Amesha Spenta nodded his head in approval.

DRAGON LORE

KATHIRESAN RAMACHANDERAM

Dragon Lore

The following excerpts have been pieced together by the dragon mages of the elven race during transcendental sleep a process which enabled them to share the consciousness of the dragons. During transcendental sleep the consciousness of the mages and the dragons merged together and their minds melded to become a single entity:-

In the beginning there was only space, dark and empty, the fabric which spanned the entire universe. The system was devoid of planets and lacked the luster of stars. Then there was a rip in the fabric of space and on the other side (the unknown)*, a tiny white light flickered, growing incessantly brighter with each passing minute. In time the tiny orbs floated through the tear, growing in size as they drifted through, like fireflies, alight with three different colors, white, yellow and red.

The white orbs grew in size to become white dwarfs, the yellow orbs grew in size to become mortal suns and the red orbs grew in size to become red giants. Each orb was in reality a minute component of the entity that had seeped through from the other side. No one has thus far ventured close enough to it to share its consciousness but all the stars

---

* *The dragon mages referred to other side as the unknown*

and the planets, every rock and crater, all things animate and inanimate in the galaxy that was known as Draganos was in actuality and in reality a part of the entity known as Dragos - the progenitor of the dragon race. Dragos spanned the entire galaxy.

Draganos was a star system unlike any other for it had more suns than it had planets, to the ratio of two to one. The planets were infinitely larger in circumference than any in the known world. On most of the planets in the Draganos system there was water and patches of greenery. There were streams, lakes and rivers filled with cool rushing liquid. Likewise there were also pools and springs of molten lava. On some of the planets there was lush green vegetation while others were left intentionally dry.

Dragos was the sole ruler and the ultimate authority in Draganos. Dragos was a solar divinity and for all purposes he was an aspect of the Brahmatma that remained unidentified. He was thought and action, contemplation and motion. Dragos had five children though some mages argue that his children were merely Dragos manifesting himself in five different forms to correspond with the five known elements: - earth, wind, water, fire and aether.

The scales on each dragon was homologous to the element that it identified with. The scales on the earth dragon were green as was its overall complexion. The wind dragon which was also known as the frost dragon had white scales. It occupied the polar ice caps on some of the lesser planets. The water dragon which inhabited the waterways and lived beneath vast expanses of water had placid blue scales. It was known as the water dragon. The red dragon that lived in volcanoes or lava filled craters had smooth red scales to match its environment. It was analogous to the fire element. Lastly there was the spirit dragon, the dragon that was synonymous to aether. Its scales were pale and it drifted with the wind like all spirits and resided on the peaks of lofty mountains.

Dragons were genderless. They reproduced only when they needed to and the mages suspected that it was Dragos who influenced a dragon's decision to multiply. Dragons laid eggs that were incubated in pools of water heated by molten lava and magma that flowed beneath.

For his dragons, Dragos created mammoth beasts to feed on, their bodies prime with juicy meat and succulent fat. He created beasts of different kinds who roamed the wide open planes. Some with horns and some without. Some of the beasts had shaggy furs while others had short mammal like coats. For these beasts he created weed that resembled exotic blades of grass that were impervious to the blistering rays of the scorching suns and water that never evaporated despite the extreme heat in pools that never needed to be replenished by rain.

In time the children of Dragos multiplied and inhabited every planet in the galaxy but their numbers were always kept to the minimal. Dragos instructed his progeny to seek knowledge and the quest for enlightenment became the sole purpose of dragon-kind.

All dragons contributed to the collective consciousness of Dragos and the solar dragon shared the memories of all dragons. It was a collective consciousness that comprised of the memories and recollections of every member of the dragon race. Dragos had access to all their memories and this reinforced the notion that each dragon was merely a different manifestation of Dragos.

Thus far this proposition has never been affirmed or repudiated for no mage has yet been able to get spiritually close enough to Dragos to access his consciousness to elucidate any information. The mages were not able to resist the brazen heat that emanated from the consciousness of Dragos for he was ablaze with the effulgence of a billion suns.

The dragons individually travelled to other planets, systems and constellations. Dragons existed as sole or individual entities and were never a part of a colony unless they were guarding a brood in which case a single dragon would remain behind to nurse the hatchlings and to stand guard over the brood.

Dragons shared an incubator and in all instances the incubator was a heated subterranean pool. Thus far the mages were unable to determine the duration of the incubation period but the mages suspected that the time frame was stipulated and manipulated by Dragos. In short the dragon population was only replenished when the need arose.

Individual dragons however shared the memories of their ancestors and therefore dragons are able to hand down their memories to their hatchlings and in this manner new hatchlings acquired the knowledge of their elders.

The mages suspected that dragon genes contained the memories of their ancestors and referred to it as genetic memory. Genetic memory alluded to the probability that dragon genes carried sequences that held within it collective memory pools located in their chromosomes.

From the genetic memories that were handed down, the mages have been able to gather that there was a time when Dragos had physically appeared to sit on the throne of Draganos located on the planet that is lighted by the dual suns, Draco Prime. The mages had glimpses of Dragos when he appeared before the ancestral dragons whose consciousness was shared by their progeny but they could only identify him as a bright white light because his personality beamed with a brilliance that was too radiant for elven eyes.

The dragons coexisted harmoniously with the feed beasts for thousands of years before there was another rip in the fabric of space and the dragons were invaded by a new race, the slithery race of serpents than in many ways resembled large eels. They fell in multitudes from the sky and dribbled into the dragon lairs in slithery torrents. The eel like serpents were winged and some had dual heads on their bodies.

These eels were sometimes called serpent-dragons simply because of their long slippery bodies and their ability to take to the sky but in reality the serpent-eels were in no way connected to the dragons. The serpent-eels were the children of the godless ones in whose vein runs the blood of that which slithers at the feet of the negative aspect of the Brahmatma.

The accursed serpent-eels varied in length and dimensions. The smaller more cunning of their race were known to be cradle snatchers that have seized thousands of infants from their cots of birth in countless planets.

The serpents multiplied rapidly occupying the underground caverns and grottos unfazed by the extremity of the heat that beat down on the surface and razed away in the interior of the planets. The serpent-eels infiltrated the dragon lairs and destroyed many of the eggs. In order to save the species, Dragos ordered that all eggs be encased in crystallized rock that was able to withstand the varying temperatures of interstellar travel and hurled into space.

Each meteor had five eggs, one for each species of dragon. It is believed that the solar dragon through its super consciousness manipulated the meteorites and directed them on trajectories that he desired plotting their course through space. Once the eggs were safely dispatched Dragos with his super consciousness made the suns of Draganos expand so that they burnt with the brilliance of a thousand suns. The surfaces of all the planets in the system were set alight with heat so intense that anything that lived was reduced to smoldering ashes within the blink of an eye.

The fires continued for a thousand years. So angered was Dragos by the intrusion that that he allowed the fires to rage unhindered and unobstructed for a hundred mortal lifetimes. Eventually his anger abated and the suns returned to their normal size but by that time all life on the planets was incinerated.

The mages believed that the home world of the dragons (Draco Prime) still existed and that the dragons can return if they wished but thus far none of the dragons that shared the consciousness of the mages had shown any signs or intentions of doing so, despite knowing its location from the charts stored in the genetic memories that they inherited from their ancestors.

In time after a journey that lasted millions of mortal years, the egg encapsulated meteors landed on earth, wedged in a shallow crater close to the edge of the sacred forest. The mages were of the belief that the selection of the site was intentional and that Dragos wanted the elves to discover the dragon eggs.

The eggs came at a time when the air was rife with white magic and every nook and cranny of the known world was glossed and tampered with enchantment that drifted upwards from open fissures and cracks on the surface like invisible vapors from the bowels of the planet at a time when elves mingled freely with mortals and there was no animosity or distrust between the races.

Then, on a bright summer morning, guided by the hand of Dawn, an elven princess, Runa of the Vale chanced to be out on her unicorn, cloud hopping when she caught sight of the crater, nestled discretely in the middle of a thick lavender bush, like a cradle encircled with flowers.

The rock was covered with a shine that made it dazzle in the morning light and the young princess could not resist taking a closer look at the strange nugget. She swooped down from the sky, astride her fleet unicorn Sir Valiant and settled her mount beside the large flowery shrub. She jumped off her horse and walked closer to the rock and as she did so, the rock started to glow.

She reached out and touched the surface of the rock and the moment it felt her touch the rock split open to reveal five eggs each the size of a full grown dwarf. Taken aback the princess sent her unicorn to call for help and soon the elf elder Nereiðr arrived in the company of a handful of elves and dwarfs with horse carts. With the help of elves and dwarfs the eggs were carefully loaded on the back of the carts and taken to Mount Kieddoaivi. There they were transported through inconspicuous passages to the underground caverns and incubated in a hot volcanic pool.

Somehow the princess knew exactly what to do with the eggs and according to her "a voice whispered in her head", giving her instructions. The mages suspected that it was the voice of Dragos but the identity of the voice was never disclosed. It would continue to speak to the princess and it appointed Runa as the maternal guardian of the eggs.

The eggs remained in incubation for almost a year and in all that time Runa kept a watchful eye on the eggs turning her back on the prospect of marriage spurning any suitor that came her way. The red dragon was the first to hatch and the princess was delighted to see the little hatchling crawl out of its egg shell. "Eat a bit of the albumen" said the voice in her head. Despite being a vegan the princess did as she was told forcing a bit of the remains from the egg shells down her throat. Within seconds she slipped into a trance and images stored in the dragon's genes flashed before her.

The green dragon was the next to hatch, followed by the blue dragon, then the white dragon and finally the pale dragon. Runa tasted a bit of the albumen from all the eggs and stored the remainder of the glair in sealed glass beakers. Thus she was able to share the memories and the consciousness of all five dragons.

The little dragons yearned for the sun and as soon as they hatched, Runa with the help of the dwarfs that worked in the caverns in the interior of the Kieddoaivi carried each of them from the underground cavern to the mouth of the cave where they could feel the sunlight touch their scales. The little dragons flapped their wings wanting to instantly fly to touch the sun and to feel its rays on their bodies but it was at least a month before they were able to take off.

Dragons she discovered were meat eaters and the infant dragon desired fresh meat as soon as it had hatched. Elves on the other hand were vegans who lived off the fruits of the valley and the nectar of the vale in addition to having a well known craving for milk and cheese.

That changed the moment she tasted the albumen in the eggs and her taste buds soon altered to follow that of the dragon. "You, dear Runa by virtue of tasting dragon blood, for the glair in the eggs contained dragon blood, become the first member of the Order of the Dragon" said the voice in her head. "From here on all mages must be initiated into the order by tasting the blood of the dragon" the voice commanded. The princess bowed her head in reply.

Meat was ordered from mortal butchers, cooked beforehand, because the princess insisted that she would not feed her children anything that was uncooked for she would not have her children develop the craving for blood or bloodlust. Bushels of roast meat were carted from villages located close to the outskirts of the sacred forest to the foot of the Kieddoaivi. The meat was fed to the hatchlings and as the dragons bit into the meat the princess felt herself sharing their bite.

That was the beginning of the merger, the melding of two minds and soon the princess would drop her elven habits and assume that of the dragons. She could feel their innermost desires and the princess through the genetic memory that all dragons inherited began unraveling the mysteries of the dragon race.

The dragons that had come to the known world belonged to a brood from a lair in the magma pits of Draco Prime and a guardian green earth dragon was appointed to watch over the eggs. It was difficult to say how long the eggs had been in incubation for.

It was the first time Runa had seen a fully grown green dragon and she was taken aback by the elegance of its flamboyant green scales. At first the dragon left the eggs unguarded and felt secure enough to frequently drift towards the sun.

Dragons fed not only on meat but on sunlight and their cells were regenerated by proximity to sunlight. For most dragons it was a daily routine. Even in the remotest corner of the far flung universe they had to come into contact with the outer crust of the sun. It was a ritual that they never ignored or forgot.

Runa soon acquired the ability to sift through the memories of the dragons with speed. As the days wore on she realized that the guardian dragon grew increasingly restless and refused to leave the side of the eggs. She saw little cracks appear on the sides of the cavern that housed the pool that doubled up as an incubator. The cracks grew larger and larger and she saw small eels slip through the cracks. The dragon let out a torrent of flame and the eels were instantly reduced to smoldering ashes but they kept reappearing falling out of the cracks onto the floor and soon the cavern was inundated with serpent-eels.

The cracks grew larger and became holes that gradually increased in circumference. The eels that slipped through swelled in size and soon resembled large slippery serpents. The serpents had large snouts and mouths filled with razor sharp teeth. Some were winged and took off to the ceiling of the cavern repeatedly attacking the dragon from all directions. The furious green dragon let out torrents of unrepentant flames and it was soon overwhelmed. It was on the verge of taking off when the voice of Dragos boomed over all else. In dragon tongue he ordered all dragons to salvage what they could and desert the planet.

The guardian dragon obeyed and gathered what eggs it could with its front paws before it flew through the wide open mouth of the volcano. For the first time Runa managed to catch a glimpse of the sky outside the natural enclosure. It was a bright yellowish-red that resembled the red twilight sky in the mortal world.

As the dragon flew over the clouds it looked downwards. The fertile green plains and valleys below were infested with the serpent-eels that fed voraciously on the beasts that were dragon feed, brutally tearing them to pieces with their razor sharp teeth and at the rate they tore the animals apart the dragons would have been starved out of existence in a matter of months. The serpent-eels were hideous to look at and the sight of them sent shivers down Runa's spine.

The dragon flew towards the mouth of another much larger volcano that looked like it had been sculpted by the hands of a master craftsman and it dropped the eggs into the mouth of the large volcano before it drifted higher into the clouds, accelerating at incredible speeds and streaked through the sky like a fiery comet. Minutes later large boulders shot out from the mouth of the volcano travelling at incredible speeds before disappearing upwards into the sky disappearing with the blink of an eye.

The sky over the horizon grew brighter and the surface was soon set alight by the radiance of a thousand suns. The serpent-eels and all life on Draco Prime was destroyed within seconds.

Once the hatchlings had gained the ability to take to the air, Dragos guided Runa again by telling her to appoint a group of five dragon mages to attend to each dragon. The selection process was difficult and the mages were selected from the ranks of elves between the ages of sixteen and eighteen. All were female. The chosen were initiated as per the instructions of the solar dragon and were made to ingest a drop of albumen that was exhumed from the shell of the dragon egg that belonged to the dragon that was allotted to them and contained the blood of the specific dragon from the vials that they were stored in.

Runa felt that females would be more motherly and more attentive to the needs of the infant dragons. Dragos, Lord Supreme of the Dragons appreciated her thoughtfulness and since the day they hatched to present the dragon mages hadn't had a single moment of un-mindful behavior from the dragons.

Elves unlike mortals were more attuned to magic being magical creatures themselves and the pathways of their minds were more susceptible to magic. They could meld more easily with other magical creatures and there was no creature in existence more magical than the dragon.

In time the mages learned of the death rites of the dragons. The dragon death rite is unique and by sharing the genetic memories that the dragons inherited, the mages learned that dragons had the ability to live for an incredibly long time and their lifespan surpassed that of even elves. In fact dragons never died and could live for as long as they wished.

Dragons perished when they chose to and at the selected time the dragon made its way to the Draganos system and searched for a suitable location. Once the dragon had found the relevant spot, it ceased eating (the lack of sustenance can lead to a dragon's demise) and   withdrew its consciousness into the deepest labyrinths of its mind. It regressed until its body ceased to be active. When it reached this point its body would start to glow and transform to become a large circular orb that burnt as radiantly as the incandescent sun eventually becoming a star that lit the endless corridors of space.

Printed in the United States
By Bookmasters